MW01671836

This

Book Belongs to

Black Beauty

BLACK BEAUTY

ANNA SEWELL

ILLUSTRATED BY LUCY KEMP-WELCH

Sandy Creek

This 2009 edition published by Sandy Creek

Sandy Creek
122 Fifth Avenue
New York, NY 10011

ISBN: 978-1-4351-1876-8

Printed and bound in the United States of America

1 3 5 7 9 10 8 6 4 2

LIST OF CHAPTERS

Part Three

Part Four

LIST OF ILLUSTRATIONS

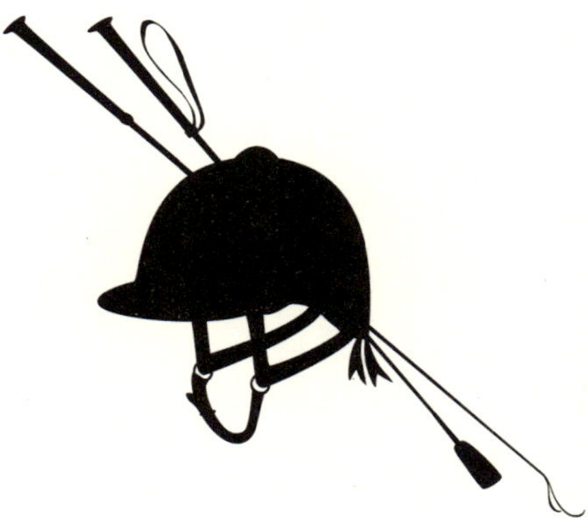

INTRODUCTION

BLACK BEAUTY IS A MAGNIFICENT TALE ABOUT A HORSE who lived during the late nineteenth century in England. It brings the reader inside the mind and heart of a noble animal and offers a unique vision of the time before automobiles and trucks, when indifferent, and sometimes cruel treatment of horses was often the norm. During this period when horses were used as the primary means of transportation, these animals endured many injustices but also met kindness at many hands.

The story is told through the perspective of Beauty and his equine friends. In a world where good and evil were easily distinguishable, Beauty's courage, fortitude, and above all his innocence, give us a lesson in the moral obligation we have to each other and to all living things. Much like the parents of a child, the "masters" have a responsibility toward the vulnerable lives under their care and protection. Beauty could neither leave his home when he was abused, nor could he speak to defend himself against injury or injustice. Because *Black*

Beauty is told from its animal protagonist's point of view, we certainly empathize with Beauty's situation. Through this process, we even recognize that this horse is a lot like us. The things that Beauty hopes for are those same intrinsic qualities of life we regard as fundamental to happiness.

Beauty begins life in untethered freedom. Before being "broken in," Beauty galloped freely in Squire Gordon's fields with no rider on his back and no burden to pull. He ate green grass when he was hungry and rested under a shady tree when he was tired. When he began his working life he began to understand how important and necessary horses were to people and this gave him a sense of pride. Because of this, he worked with much diligence and patience. Yet, in return he was given little understanding and, too often, given the whip. His liberty became only a memory—but the wish to taste it again kept him strong during his bleakest times.

In 1877, the year of *Black Beauty*'s publication, it was the fashion in England to make horses hold their heads as high as possible when they were in public, regardless of the weight the animal was pulling or the steepness of the incline being negotiated. Since this extreme position was unnatural to the horse, the bearing rein was used. This rein kept the horse's head straining upright, causing him to foam at the mouth, as well as making it difficult for him to breathe. Over time the pressure of the bearing rein taxed a horse so greatly that he often became too ill to perform his duties. The dire consequences of this fashion fell entirely on the horses.

Beauty worked at many different occupations throughout his life, among them carriage horse, cab horse, and cart horse. The treatment he received was as varied as his jobs and masters were. Like all beasts of burden, Beauty had to rely on the goodness of his owners and grooms for his safety and well-being. Through all his experiences, the indignities as well as the kindnesses, at the mercy of spiteful enemies or during a relief, thanks to constant friends, Beauty's behavior was a testimony to grace and dignity.

Beauty's is an unforgettable voice, inspired both by kindness and injustice, a voice that speaks for horse and human alike.

—GAIL DOOBININ

1994

Part One

CHAPTER I

My Early Home

THE FIRST PLACE THAT I CAN WELL REMEMBER was a large pleasant meadow with a pond of clear water in it. Some shady trees leaned over it, and rushes and water-lilies grew at the deep end. Over the hedge on one side we looked into a plowed field, and on the other we looked over a gate at our master's house, which stood by the roadside. At the top of the meadow was a plantation of fir trees, and at the bottom a running brook overhung by a steep bank.

While I was young I lived upon my mother's milk, as I could not eat grass. In the daytime I ran by her side, and at night I lay down close by her. When it was hot we used to stand by the pond in the shade of the trees, and when it was cold we had a warm shed near the grove.

As soon as I was old enough to eat grass, my mother used to go out to work in the daytime, and come back in the evening.

There were six young colts in the meadow besides me. They were older than I was; some were nearly as large as grown-up horses. I used to run with them, and had great fun; we used to gallop all together round and round the field, as hard as we could go. Sometimes we had rather rough play, for they would frequently bite and kick, as well as gallop.

One day, when there was a good deal of kicking, my mother whinnied to me to come to her, and then she said:

"I wish you to pay attention to what I am going to say to you. The colts who live here are very good colts, but they are cart-horse colts and, of course, they have not learned manners. You have been well-bred and well-born; your father has a great name in these parts, and your grandfather won the cup two years at the Newmarket races; your grandmother had the sweetest temper of any horse I ever knew, and I think you have never seen me kick or bite. I hope you will grow up gentle and good, and never learn bad ways; do your work with a good will, lift your feet up well when you trot, and never bite or kick even in play."

I have never forgotten my mother's advice. I knew she was a wise old horse, and our master thought a great deal of her. Her name was Duchess, but he often called her Pet.

Our master was a good, kind man. He gave us good food, good lodging, and kind words; he spoke as kindly to us as he did to his little children. We were all fond of him, and my mother loved him very much. When she saw him at the gate, she would neigh with joy, and trot up to him. He would pat and stroke her and say, "Well, old Pet, and how is your little Darkie?" I was a dull black, so he called me Darkie, then he would give me a piece of bread, which was very good, and sometimes he brought a carrot for my mother. All the horses would come to him, but I think we were his favorites. My mother always took him to the town on a market-day in a light gig.

There was a plowboy, Dick, who sometimes came into our field to pluck blackberries from the hedge. When he had eaten all he wanted he would have what he called fun with the colts, throwing stones and sticks at them to make them gallop. We did not much mind him, for we could gallop off, but sometimes a stone would hit and hurt us.

One day he was at this game, and did not know that the master was in the next field, but he was there, watching what was going on. Over the hedge he jumped in a snap, and catching Dick by the arm, he gave him such a box on the ear as made him roar with the pain and surprise. As soon as we saw the master, we trotted up nearer to see what went on.

"Bad boy!" he said. "Bad boy to chase the colts! This is not the first time, nor the second, but it shall be the last. There—take your money and go home; I shall not want you on my farm again." So we never saw Dick any more. Old Daniel, the man who looked after the horses, was just as gentle as our master, so we were well off.

CHAPTER II

The Hunt

BEFORE I WAS TWO YEARS OLD A CIRCUMSTANCE happened which I have never forgotten. It was early in the spring; there had been a little frost in the night, and a light mist still hung over the woods and meadows. I and the other colts were feeding at the lower part of the field when we heard, quite in the distance, what sounded like the cry of dogs. The oldest of the colts raised his head, pricked his ears, and said, "There are the hounds!" and immediately cantered off, followed by the rest of us to the upper part of the field, where we could look over the hedge and see several fields beyond. My mother and an old riding horse of our master's were also standing near, and seemed to know all about it.

"They have found a hare," said my mother, "and if they come this way we shall see the hunt."

And soon the dogs were all tearing down the field of young wheat next to ours. I never heard such a noise as they made. They did not bark, nor howl, nor whine, but kept on a "yo! yo, o, o! yo! yo, o, o!" at the top of their voices. After them came a number of men on horseback, some of them in green coats, all galloping as fast as they could. The old horses snorted and looked eagerly after them, but they were soon away into the fields lower down; here it seemed as if they had come to a stand; the dogs left off barking and ran about every way with their noses to the ground.

"They have lost the scent," said the old horse; "perhaps the hare will get off."

"What hare?" I said.

"Oh! I don't know *what* hare; likely enough it may be one of our own hares out of the woods; any hare they can find will do for the dogs and men to run after." And before long the dogs began their "yo! yo, o, o!" again, and back they came all together at full speed, making straight for our meadow at the part where the high bank and hedge overhang the brook.

"Now we shall see the hare," said my mother, and just then a hare, wild with fright, rushed by and made for the woods. On came the dogs; they burst over the bank, leaped the stream, and came dashing across the field, followed by the huntsmen. Six or eight men leaped their horses clean over, close upon the dogs. The hare tried to get through the fence; it was too thick, and she turned sharp round to make for the road, but it was too late; the dogs were upon her with their wild cries. We heard one shriek, and that was the end of her. One of the huntsmen rode up and whipped off the dogs, who would soon have torn her to pieces. He held her up by the leg, torn and bleeding, *and all the gentlemen seemed well pleased.*

As for me, I was so astonished that I did not at first see what was going on by the brook; but when I did look, there was a sad sight. Two fine horses were down; one was struggling in the stream, and the other was groaning on the grass. One of the riders was getting out of the water covered with mud, the other lay quite still.

"His neck is broken," said my mother.

"And serves him right, too," said one of the colts.

I thought the same, but my mother did not join with us.

"Well, no," she said, "you must not say that. But though I am an old horse and have seen and heard a great deal, I never yet could make out why men are so fond of this sport; they often hurt themselves, often spoil good horses, and tear up the fields, and all for a hare or a fox, or a stag, that they could get more easily some other way; but we are only horses, and don't know."

While my mother was saying this, we stood and looked on. Many of the riders had gone to the young man; but my master, who had been watching what was going on, was the first to raise him. His head fell back and his arms hung down, and everyone looked very serious. *There was no noise now; even the dogs were quiet, and seemed to know that something was wrong. They carried him to our master's house.* I heard afterward that it was young George Gordon, the squire's only son, a fine, tall young man, and the pride of his family.

They were now riding in all directions—to the doctor's, to the farrier's, and no doubt to Squire Gordon's, to let him know about his son. When Mr. Bond, the farrier, came to look at the black horse that lay groaning on the grass, he felt him all over, and shook his head; one of his legs was broken. Then someone ran to our master's house and came back with a gun. Presently there was a loud bang and a dreadful shriek, and then all was still; the black horse moved no more.

My mother seemed much troubled. She said she had known that horse for years, and that his name was "Rob Roy"; he was a good horse, and there was no vice in him. She never would go to that part of the field afterward.

Not many days after, we heard the church-bell tolling for a long time, and looking over the gate, we saw a long, strange black coach that was covered with black cloth and was drawn by black horses. After that came another and another and another, and all were black, while the bell kept tolling, tolling. *They were carrying young Gordon to the church-yard to bury him. He would never ride again. What they did with Rob Roy I never knew, but 'twas all for one little hare.*

CHAPTER III

My Breaking In

I WAS NOW BEGINNING TO GROW HANDSOME; MY COAT had grown fine and soft, and was bright black. I had one white foot, and a pretty white star on my forehead. I was thought very handsome. My master would not sell me till I was four years old; he said lads ought not to work like men, and colts ought not work like horses till they were quite grown up.

When I was four years old, Squire Gordon came to look at me. He examined my eyes, my mouth, and my legs; he felt them all down, and then I had to walk and trot and gallop before him. He seemed to like me, and said, "When he has been well broken in, he will do very well." My master said he would break me in himself, as he should not like me to be frightened or hurt, and he lost no time about it, for the next day he began.

Everyone may not know what breaking in is, therefore I will describe it. It means to teach a horse to wear a saddle and bridle, and to carry on his back a man, woman, or child; to go just the way they wish, and to go quietly. Besides this, he has to learn to wear a collar, a crupper, and a breeching, and to stand still while they are put on; then to have a cart or a chaise fixed behind him, so that he cannot walk or trot without dragging it after him. And he must go fast or slow, just as his driver wishes. He must never start at what he sees, nor speak to other horses, nor bite, nor kick, nor have any will of his own; but always do his master's will, even though he may be very tired or hungry. But the worst of all is, when his harness is once on, he may neither jump for joy nor lie down for weariness. So you see this breaking in is a great thing.

I had, of course, long been used to a halter and a headstall, and to be led about in the field and lanes quietly, but now I was to have a bit and a bridle. My master gave me some oats as usual, and after a good deal of coaxing he got the bit into my mouth, and the bridle fixed, but it was a nasty thing! Those who have never had a bit in their mouths cannot think how bad it feels; a great piece of cold hard steel as thick as a man's finger to be pushed into one's mouth, between one's teeth and over one's tongue, with the ends coming out at the corners of your mouth, and held fast there by straps over your head, under your throat, round your nose, and under your chin; so that in no way in the world can you get rid of the nasty hard thing. It is very bad! Yes, very bad! At least I thought so; but I knew my mother always wore one when she went out, and all horses did when they were grown up. And so, what with the nice oats, and with my master's pats, kind words, and gentle ways, I got to wear my bit and bridle.

Next came the saddle, but that was not half so bad. My master put it on my back very gently while old Daniel held my head; he then made the girths fast under my body, patting and talking to me all the time. Then I had a few oats, then a little leading about, and this he did every day till I began to look for the oats and the saddle. At length, one morning my master got on my back and rode me round the meadow on the soft grass. It certainly did feel queer. But I must say I felt rather proud to carry my master, and as he continued to ride me a little every day I soon became accustomed to it.

The next unpleasant business was putting on the iron shoes; that too was very hard at first. My master went with me to the smith's forge, to see that I was not hurt or got any fright. The blacksmith took my feet in his hand one after the other, and cut away some of the hoof. It did not pain me, so I stood still on three legs till he had done them all. Then he took a piece of iron the shape of my foot and clapped it on, and drove some nails through the shoe quite into my hoof, so that the shoe was firmly on. My feet felt very stiff and heavy, but in time I got used to it.

And now having got so far, my master went on to break me to harness. There were more new things to wear. First, a stiff heavy collar just on my neck, and a bridle with great side-pieces against my eyes, called blinkers, and blinkers indeed they were, for I could not see on either side but only straight in front of me. Next there was a small saddle with a nasty stiff strap that went right under my tail. That was the crupper. I hated the crupper—to have my long tail doubled up and poked through that strap was almost as bad as the bit. I never felt more like kicking, but of course I could not kick such a good master, and so in time I got used to everything and could do my work as well as my mother.

I must not forget to mention one part of my training which I have always considered a very great advantage. My master sent me for a fortnight to a neighboring farmer's, who had a meadow which was skirted on one side by the railway. Here were some sheep and cows, and I was turned in among them.

I shall never forget the first train that ran by. I was feeding quietly near the pales which separated the meadow from the railway, when I heard a strange sound at a distance, and before I knew whence it came—with a rush and a clatter, and a puffing out of smoke—a long black train of something flew by, and was gone almost before I could draw my breath. I turned and galloped to the further side of the meadow as fast as I could go, and there I stood snorting with astonishment and fear. In the course of the day many other trains went by, some more slowly. These drew up at the station close by and sometimes made an awful shriek and groan before they stopped. I thought it very dreadful, but the cows went on eating very quietly and hardly raised their heads as the black, frightful thing came puffing and grinding past. For the first few days I could not feed in peace; but as I found that this terrible creature never came into the field, or did me any harm, I began to disregard it, and very soon I cared as little about the passing of a train as the cows and sheep did.

Since then I have seen many horses much alarmed and restive at the sight or sound of a steam engine; but thanks to my good master's care, I am as fearless at railway stations as in my own stable.

Now if anyone wants to break in a young horse well, that is the way.

My master often drove me in double harness, with my mother, because she was steady and could teach me how to go better than a strange horse. She told me the better I behaved the better I should be treated, and that it was wisest always to do my best to please my master. “But,” said she, “there are a great many kinds of men: there are good, thoughtful men like our master that any horse may be proud to serve, but there are bad, cruel men who never ought to have a horse or dog to call their own. Besides, there are a great many foolish men, vain, ignorant and careless, who never trouble themselves to think. These spoil more horses than all, just for want of sense; they don’t mean it, but they do it for all that. I hope you will fall into good hands, but a horse never knows who may buy him, or who may drive him. It is all a chance for us; but still I say, do your best wherever it is, and keep up your good name.”

CHAPTER IV

Birtwick Park

At this time I used to stand in the stable, and my coat was brushed every day till it shone like a rook's wing. It was early in May, when there came a man from Squire Gordon's who took me away to the Hall. My master said, "Good-bye, Darkie, be a good horse and always do your best." I could not say "Good-bye," so I put my nose into his hand. He patted me kindly, and I left my first home. As I lived some years with Squire Gordon, I may as well tell something about the place.

Squire Gordon's park skirted the village of Birtwick. It was entered by a large iron gate, at which stood the first lodge, and then you trotted along on a smooth road between clumps of large old trees; then another lodge and another gate, which brought you to the house and the gardens. Beyond this lay the home paddock, the old orchard, and the stables. There was accommodation for many horses and carriages, but I need only describe the stable into which I was taken. This was very roomy, with four good stalls. A large swinging window opened into the yard, which made it pleasant and airy.

The first stall was a large square one, shut in behind with a wooden gate. The others were common stalls, good stalls, but not nearly so large. It had a low rack for hay and a low manger for corn; it was called a loose box, because the horse that was put into it was not tied up, but left loose, to do as he liked. It is a great thing to have a loose box.

Into this fine box the groom put me. It was clean, sweet and airy. I never was in a better box than that, and the sides were not so high but that I could see all that went on through the iron rails that were at the top.

He gave me some very nice oats, he patted me, spoke kindly, and then went away.

When I had eaten my corn I looked around. In the stall next to mine stood a little fat gray pony, with a thick mane and tail, a very pretty head and a pert little nose.

I put my head up to the iron rails at the top of my box and said, "How do you do? What is your name?"

He turned around as far as his halter would allow, held up his head, and said, "My name is Merrylegs. I am very handsome. I carry the young ladies on my back, and sometimes I take our mistress out in the low chaise. They think a great deal of me, and so does James. Are you going to live next door to me in the box?"

I said, "Yes."

"Well, then," he said, "I hope you are good-tempered. I do not like anyone next door who bites."

Just then a horse's head looked over from the stall beyond; the ears were laid back, and the eye looked rather ill-tempered. This was a tall chestnut mare with a long, handsome neck. She looked across to me and said:

"So it is you who have turned me out of my box. It is a very strange thing for a colt like you to come and turn a lady out of her own home."

"I beg your pardon," I said, "I have turned no one out. The man who brought me put me here, and I had nothing to do with it; and as to my being a colt, I am turned four years old and am a grown-up horse. I never had words yet with horse or mare, and it is my wish to live at peace."

"Well," she said, "we shall see; I do not want to have words with a young thing like you."

I said no more.

In the afternoon when she went out, Merrylegs told me all about it.

"The thing is this," said Merrylegs, "Ginger has a bad habit of biting and snapping. That is why they call her Ginger, and when she was in the loose box she used to snap very much. One day she bit James in the arm and made it bleed, and so Miss Flora and Miss Jessie, who are very fond of me, were afraid to come into the stable. They used to bring me nice things to eat, an apple or a carrot, or a piece of bread, but after Ginger stood in that box they dared not come, and I missed them very much. I hope they will now come again, if you do not bite or snap."

I told him I never bit anything but grass, hay and corn, and could not think what pleasure Ginger found in it.

"Well, I don't think she does find pleasure," said Merrylegs. "It is just a bad habit. She says no one was ever kind to her, and why should she not bite? Of course it is a very bad habit, but I am sure if all she says be true, she must have been very ill-used before she came here. John does all he can to please her, and James does all he can, and our master never uses a whip if a horse acts right, so I think she might be good-tempered here. You see," he said with a wise look, "I am twelve years old, I know a great deal, and I can tell you there is not a better place for a horse all round the country than this. John is the best groom that ever was; he has been here fourteen years; and you never saw such a kind boy as James is; so that it is all Ginger's own fault that she did not stay in that box."

CHAPTER V

A Fair Start

THE NAME OF THE COACHMAN WAS JOHN MANLY. He had a wife and one little child, and they lived in the coachman's cottage, very near the stables.

The next morning he took me into the yard and gave me a good grooming, and just as I was going into my box, with my coat soft and bright, the Squire came in to look at me, and seemed pleased. "John," he said, "I meant to have tried the new horse this morning, but I have other business. You may as well take him around after breakfast; go by the common and the Highwood, and back by the water mill and the river. That will show his paces."

"I will, sir," said John. After breakfast he came and fitted me with a bridle. He was very particular in letting out and taking in the straps to fit my head comfortably. Then he brought a saddle, but it was not broad enough for my back; he saw it in a minute and went for another, which fitted nicely. He rode me first slowly, then a trot, then a canter, and when we were on the common he gave me a light touch with his whip, and we had a splendid gallop.

"Ho, ho, my boy," he said as he pulled me up, "you would like to follow the hounds, I think."

As we came back through the Park we met the Squire and Mrs. Gordon walking; they stopped, and John jumped off.

"Well, John, how does he go?"

"First-rate, sir," answered John. "He is as fleet as a deer, and has a fine spirit too, but the lightest touch of the rein will guide him. Down at the end of the common we met one of those traveling carts hung all over with baskets, rugs, and such like. You know, sir, many horses will not pass those carts quietly. He just took a good look at it, and then went on as quiet and pleasant as could be. They were shooting rabbits near the Highwood, and a gun went off close by. He pulled up a little and looked, but did not stir a step to right or left. I just held the rein steady and did not hurry him, and it's my opinion he has not been frightened or ill-used while he was young."

"That's well," said the Squire, "I will try him myself tomorrow."

The next day I was brought up for my master. I remembered my mother's counsel and my good old master's, and tried to do exactly what he wanted me to do. I found he was a very good rider, and thoughtful for his horse, too. When he came home, the lady was at the hall door as he rode up.

"Well, my dear," she said, "how do you like him?"

"He is exactly what John said," he replied. "A pleasanter creature I never wish to mount. What shall we call him?"

"Would you like Ebony?" said she. "He is as black as ebony."

"No, not Ebony."

"Will you call him Blackbird, like your uncle's old horse?"

"No, he is far handsomer than old Blackbird ever was."

"Yes," she said, "he is really quite a beauty, and he has such a sweet, good-tempered face and such a fine, intelligent eye—What do you say to calling him *Black Beauty?*"

"Black Beauty—Why, yes, I think that is a very good name. If you like, it shall be his name." And so it was.

When John went into the stable, he told James that master and mistress had chosen a good, sensible name for me, that meant something—not like Marengo, or Pegasus, or Abdallah. They both laughed, and James said, "If it was not for bringing back the past, I should have named him Rob Roy, for I never saw two horses more alike."

"That's no wonder," said John. "Didn't you know that Farmer Grey's old Duchess was the mother of them both?"

I had never heard of that before, and *so poor Rob Roy, who was killed at the hunt, was my brother!* I did not wonder that my mother was so troubled. It seems that horses have no relations; at least they never know each other after they are sold.

John seemed very proud of me. He used to make my mane and tail almost as smooth as a lady's hair, and he would talk to me a great deal. Of course I did not understand all he said, but I learned more and more to know what he *meant,* and what he wanted me to do. *I grew very fond of him, he was so gentle and kind. He seemed to know just how a horse feels, and when he cleaned me he knew the tender places, and the ticklish places. When he brushed my head, he went as carefully over my eyes as if they were his own, and never stirred up any ill temper.*

James Howard, the stable boy, was just as gentle and pleasant in his way, so I thought myself well off. There was another man who helped in the yard, but he had very little to do with Ginger and me.

A few days after this I had to go out with Ginger in the carriage. I wondered how we should get on together, but except for laying her ears back when I was led up to her, she behaved very well. She did her work honestly, and did her full share, and I never wish to have a better partner in double harness. When we came to a hill, instead of slackening her pace, she would throw her weight right into the collar, and pull away straight up. We both had the same sort of courage at our work, and John had oftener to hold us in than to urge us forward; he never had to use the whip with either of us. Then our paces were much the same, and I found it very easy to keep step with her when trotting, which made it pleasant, and master always liked it when we kept step well, and so did John. After we had been out two or three times together we grew quite friendly and sociable, which made me feel very much at home.

As for Merrylegs, he and I soon became good friends. He was such a cheerful, plucky, good-tempered little fellow that he was a favorite with everyone, and especially with Miss Jessie and Flora, who used to ride him about in the orchard, and have fine games with him and their little dog, Frisky.

Our master had two other horses that stood in another stable. One was Justice, a roan cob, used for riding, or for the luggage cart. The other was an old brown hunter named Sir Oliver. He was past work now, but was a great favorite with the master, who gave him the run of the park. He sometimes did a little light carrying on the estate, or carried one of the young ladies when they rode out with their father, for he was gentle and could be trusted with a child as well as Merrylegs. The cob was a strong, well-made, good-tempered horse, and we sometimes had a little chat in the paddock, but of course I could not be so intimate with him as with Ginger, who stood in the same stable.

CHAPTER VI

Liberty

I WAS QUITE HAPPY IN MY NEW PLACE, AND IF THERE was one thing that I missed, it must not be thought I was discontented. All who had to do with me were good, and I had a light, airy stable and the best of food. What more could I want? Why, liberty! For three years and a half of my life I had had all the liberty I could wish for; but now, week after week, month after month, and no doubt year after year, I must stand up in a stable night and day except when I am wanted, and then I must be just as steady and quiet as any old horse who has worked twenty years. Straps here and straps there, a bit in my mouth, and blinkers over my eyes. Now, I am not complaining, for I know it must be so. I only mean to say that for a young horse full of strength and spirits, who has been used to some large field or plain, where he can fling up his head, and toss up his tail and gallop away at full speed, then round and back again with a snort to his companions—I say it is hard never to have a bit more liberty to do as you like. Sometimes, when I have had less exercise than usual, I have felt so full of life and spring that when John took me out to exercise I really could not keep quiet. Do what I would, it seemed as if I must jump, or dance, or prance, and many a good shake I know I must have given him, especially at the first, but he was always good and patient.

"Steady, steady, my boy," he would say. "Wait a bit, and we'll have a good swing and soon get the tickle out of your feet." Then as soon as we were out of the village he would give me a few miles at a spanking trot, and then bring me back as fresh as before, only clear of the fidgets, as he called them. *Spirited horses, when not enough exercised, are often called skittish,* when it is only play, and some grooms will punish them. But our John did not; he knew it was only high spirits. Still, he had his own ways of making me understand by the tone of his voice or the touch of the rein. If he was very serious and quite determined, I always knew it by his voice, and that had more power with me than anything else, for I was very fond of him.

I ought to say that sometimes we had our liberty for a few hours. This used to be on fine Sundays in the summertime. The carriage never went out on Sundays because the church was not far off.

It was a great treat to us to be turned out into the home paddock or the old orchard. The grass was so cool and soft to our feet, the air so sweet, and the freedom to do as we liked was so pleasant—to gallop, to lie down and roll over on our backs, or to nibble the sweet grass. Then it was a very good time for talking, as we stood together under the shade of the large chestnut-tree.

CHAPTER VII

Ginger

ONE DAY WHEN GINGER AND I WERE STANDING alone in the shade we had a great deal of talk. She wanted to know all about my bringing up and breaking in, and I told her.

"Well," she said, "*If I had had your bringing up, I might have had as good a temper as you,* but now I don't believe I ever shall."

"Why not?" I said.

"Because it has been all so different with me," she replied. "*I never had anyone, horse or man, that was kind to me,* or that I cared to please, for in the first place I was taken from my mother as soon as I was weaned and put with a lot of other young colts. None of them cared for me, and I cared for none of them. There was no kind master like yours to look after me, and talk to me, and bring me nice things to eat. *The man that had the care of us never gave me a kind word in my life.* I do not mean that he ill-used me, but he did not care for us one bit further than to see that we had plenty to eat and shelter in the winter. A footpath ran through our field, and very often the great boys passing through would fling stones to make us gallop. I was never hit, but one fine young colt was badly cut in the face, and I should think it would be a scar for life. We did not care for them, but of course it made us more wild, and we settled it in our minds that boys were our enemies. We had very good fun in the free meadows, galloping up and down and chasing each other round and round the field, then standing still under the shade of the trees. But when it came to breaking in, that was a bad time for me. Several men came to catch me, and when at last they closed me in at one corner of the field, one caught me by the forelock, another caught me by the nose and held it so tight I could hardly draw my breath. Then another took my underjaw in his hard hand and wrenched my mouth open, and so by force they got on the halter and the bar into my mouth. Then one dragged me along by the halter, another flogging behind, and this was the first experience I had of men's kindness—it was all force. They did not give me a chance to know what they wanted. I was high-bred and had a great deal of spirit, and was very wild, no doubt, and gave them, I dare say, plenty of trouble. But then it was dreadful to be shut up in a stall day after day instead of having my liberty, and I fretted and pined and wanted to get loose. You know yourself it's bad enough when you have a kind master and plenty of coaxing, but there was nothing of that sort for me.

"There was one—the old master, Mr. Ryder—who I think could soon have brought me around, and could have done anything with me, but he had given up all the hard part of the trade to his son and to another experienced man, and he only came at times to oversee. His son was a strong, tall, bold man; they called him Samson, and he used to boast that he had never found a horse that could throw him. There was no gentleness in him, as there was in his father, but only hardness, a hard voice, a hard eye, a hard hand, and I felt from the first that what he wanted was to wear all the spirit out of me, and just make me into a quiet, humble, obedient piece of horseflesh. 'Horse-flesh!' Yes, that is all that he thought about." And Ginger stamped her foot as if the very thought of him made her angry. Then she went on:

"If I did not do exactly what he wanted, he would get put out and make me run around with that long rein in the training field till he had tired me out. I think he drank a good deal, and I am quite sure that the oftener he drank, the worse it was for me. One day he had worked me hard in every way he could, and when I lay down I was tired and miserable and angry; it all seemed so hard. The next morning he came for me early, and ran me round again for a long time. I had scarcely had an hour's rest when he came again for me with a saddle and bridle and a new kind of bit. I could never quite tell how it came about; he had only just mounted me on the training ground, when something I did put him out of temper, and he chucked me hard with the rein. The new bit was very painful, and I reared up suddenly, which angered him still more, and he began to flog me. I felt my whole spirit set against him, and I began to kick, and plunge, and rear as I had never done before, and we had a regular fight. For a long time he stuck to the saddle and punished me cruelly with his whip and spurs, but my blood was thoroughly up, and I cared for nothing he could do if only I could get him off. At last, after a terrible struggle, I threw him off backwards. I heard him fall heavily on the turf, and without looking behind me, I galloped off to the other end of the field. There I turned around and saw my persecutor slowly rising from the ground and going into the stable. I stood under an oak tree and watched, but no one came to catch me. The time went on, the sun was very hot; the flies swarmed round me and settled on my bleeding flanks where the spurs had dug in. I felt hungry, for I had not eaten since the early morning, but there was not enough grass in that meadow for a goose to live on. I wanted to lie down and rest, but with the saddle strapped tightly on there was no comfort, and there was not a drop of water to drink. The afternoon wore on, and the sun got low. I saw the other colts led in, and I knew they were having a good feed.

"At last, just as the sun went down, I saw the old master come out with a sieve in his hand. He was a very fine old gentleman with quite white hair, but his voice was what I should know him by amongst a thousand. It was not high, nor yet low, but full, and clear, and kind, and when he gave orders it was so steady and decided that everyone knew, both horses and men, that he expected to be obeyed. He came quietly along, now and then shaking the oats about that he had in the sieve, and speaking cheerfully and gently to me: 'Come along, lassie, come along, lassie; come along, come along.' I stood still and let him come up. He held the oats to me and I began to eat without fear; his voice took all my fear away. He stood by, patting and stroking me while I was eating, and seeing the clots of blood on my side, he seemed very vexed. 'Poor lassie! It was a bad business, a bad business!' Then he quietly took the rein and led me to the stable.

"Just at the door stood Samson. I laid my ears back and snapped at him. 'Stand back,' said the master, 'and keep out of her way; you've done a bad day's work for this filly.' He growled out something about a vicious brute. 'Hark ye,' said the father, 'a bad-tempered man will never make a good-tempered horse. You've not learned your trade yet, Samson.' Then he led me into my box, took off the saddle and bridle with his own hands, and tied me up. Then he called for a pail of warm water and a sponge, took off his coat, and while the stableman held the pail, he sponged my sides a good while, so tenderly that I was sure he knew how sore and bruised they were. 'Whoa, my pretty one!' he said. 'Stand still, stand still.' *His very voice did me good,* and the bathing was very comfortable. The skin was so broken at the corners of my mouth that I could not eat the hay, the stalks hurt me. He looked closely at it, shook his head, and told the man to fetch a good bran mash and put some meal into it. How good that mash was! And so soft and healing to my mouth. He stood by all the time I was eating, stroking me and talking to the man. 'If a high-mettled creature like this,' said he, 'can't be broken in by fair means, she will never be good for anything.'

"After that he often came to see me, and when my mouth was healed, the other breaker—Job, they called him—went on training me. He was steady and thoughtful, and I soon learned what he wanted."

CHAPTER VIII

Ginger's Story Continued

THE NEXT TIME THAT GINGER AND I WERE TOGETHER in the paddock, she told me about her first place.

"After my breaking in," she said, "I was bought by a dealer to match another chestnut horse. For some weeks he drove us together, and then we were sold to a fashionable gentleman and were sent up to London. I had been driven with a check-rein by the dealer, and I hated it worse than anything else; but in this place we were reined far tighter, the coachman and his master thinking we looked more stylish so. We were often driven about in the park and other fashionable places. You who never had a check-rein on don't know what it is, but I can tell you it is dreadful.

"I like to toss my head about, and hold it as high as any horse. But fancy now yourself, if you tossed your head up high, *and were obliged to hold it there, and that for hours together, not able to move it at all except with a jerk still higher, your neck aching till you did not know how to bear it.* Besides that, to have two bits instead of one, and mine was a sharp one; it hurt my tongue and my jaw, and the blood from my tongue colored the froth that kept flying from my lips, as I chafed and fretted at the bits and rein. *It was worse when we had to stand by the hour waiting for our mistress at some grand party or entertainment;* and if I fretted or stamped with impatience the whip was laid on. It was enough to drive one mad."

"Did not your master take any thought for you?" I said.

"No," said she, "he only cared to have a stylish turnout, as they called it. I think he knew very little about horses; he left that to his coachman, who told him I had an irritable temper, that I had not been well broken to the check-rein, but I should soon get used to it. But *he* was not the man to do it, for when I was in the stable, miserable and angry, instead of being soothed and quieted by kindness, I got only a surly word or a blow. If he had been civil, I would have tried to bear it. I was willing to work, and ready to work hard, too; but to be tormented for nothing but their fancies angered me. What right had they to make me suffer like that? Besides the soreness in my mouth and the pain in my neck, *it always made my windpipe feel bad,* and if I had stopped there long I know it would have spoiled my breathing. But I grew more and more restless and irritable, I could not help it, and I began to snap and kick when anyone came to harness me. For this the groom beat me, and one day, as they had just buckled us into the carriage and were straining my head up with that rein, I began to plunge and kick with all my might. I soon broke a lot of harness, and kicked myself clear; so that was an end of that place.

"After this, I was sent to Tattersall's to be sold. Of course I could not be warranted free from vice, so nothing was said about that.

My handsome appearance and good paces soon brought a gentleman to bid for me, and I was bought by another dealer. He tried me in all kinds of ways and with different bits, and soon found out what I could bear. At last he drove me quite without a check-rein, and then sold me as a perfectly quiet horse to a gentleman in the country. He was a good master, and I was getting on very well, but his old groom left him and a new one came. This man was as hard-tempered and hard-handed as Samson. *He always spoke in a rough, impatient voice,* and if I did not move in the stall the moment he wanted me, he would hit me above the hocks with his stable broom or the fork, whichever he might have in his hand. Everything he did was rough, and I began to hate him. He wanted to make me afraid of him, but I was too high-mettled for that, and one day when he had aggravated me more than usual, I bit him, which of course put him in a great rage, and he began to hit me about the head with a riding whip. After that, he never dared to come into my stall again; either my heels or my teeth were ready for him, and he knew it. I was quite quiet with my master, but of course he listened to what the man said, and so I was sold again.

"The same dealer heard of me, and said he thought he knew one place where I should do well. ' 'Twas a pity,' he said, 'that such a fine horse should go to the bad for want of a real good chance,' and the end of it was that I came here not long before you did. But I had then made up my mind that men were my natural enemies and that I must defend myself. Of course it is very different here, but who knows how long it will last? I wish I could think about things as you do, but I can't after all I have gone through."

"Well," I said, "I think it would be a real shame if you were to bite or kick John or James."

"I don't mean to," she said, "while they are good to me. I did bite James once pretty sharp, but John said, 'Try her with kindness,' and instead of punishing me as I expected, James came to me with his arm bound up, and brought me a bran mash and stroked me. And I have never snapped at him since, and I won't either."

I was sorry for Ginger, but of course I knew very little then, and I thought most likely she made the worst of it. However, I found that as the weeks went on, she grew much more gentle and cheerful, and had lost the watchful, defiant look that she used to turn on any strange person who came near her. And one day James said, "I do believe that mare is getting fond of me, she quite whinnied after me this morning when I had been rubbing her forehead."

"Aye, aye, Jim, 'tis *'the Birtwick horse-balls,'*" said John. "She'll be as good as Black Beauty by and by. Kindness is all the physic she wants, poor thing!" Master noticed the change too, and one day when he got out of the carriage and came to speak to us, as he often did, he stroked her beautiful neck. "Well, my pretty one, well, how do things go with you now? You are a good bit happier than when you came to us, I think."

She put her nose up to him in a friendly, trustful way while he rubbed it gently.

"We shall make a cure of her, John," he said.

"Yes, sir, she's wonderfully improved; she's not the same creature that she was. It's *'the Birtwick balls,'* sir," said John, laughing.

This was a little joke of John's. He used to say that a regular course of *"the Birtwick horse-balls"* would cure almost any vicious horse. These balls, he said, were made up *of patience and gentleness, firmness and petting; one pound of each to be mixed up with half a pint of common-sense, and given to the horse every day.*

CHAPTER IX

Merrylegs

THE VICAR, MR. BLOOMFIELD, HAD A LARGE FAMILY of boys and girls. Sometimes they used to come and play with Miss Jessie and Flora. One of the girls was as old as Miss Jessie; two of the boys were older, and there were several little ones. When they came there was plenty of work for Merrylegs, for nothing pleased them so much as getting on him by turns and riding him all about the orchard and the home paddock, and this they would do by the hour together.

One afternoon he had been out with them a long time, and when James brought him in and put on his halter, he said:

"There, you rogue, mind how you behave yourself, or we shall get into trouble."

"What have you been doing, Merrylegs?" I asked.

"Oh!" said he, tossing his little head. "I have only been giving those young people a lesson. They did not know when they had

had enough, nor when I had had enough, so I just pitched them off backwards; that was the only thing they could understand."

"What?" said I. "You threw the children off? I thought you did know better than that! Did you throw Miss Jessie or Miss Flora?"

He looked very much offended, and said:

"Of course not, I would not do such a thing for the best oats that ever came into the stable. Why, I am as careful of our young ladies as the master could be, and as for the little ones, it is I who teaches them to ride. When they seem frightened or a little unsteady on my back, I go as smooth and as quiet as old pussy when she is after a bird, and when they are all right, I go on faster, you see, just to use them to it. So don't you trouble yourself preaching to me. I am the best friend and the best riding master those children have. It is not them, it is the boys; boys," said he, shaking his mane, "are quite different, they must be broken in, as we were broken in when we were colts, and just be taught what's what.

"The other children had ridden me about for nearly two hours, and then the boys thought it was their turn, and so it was, and I was quite agreeable. They rode me by turns, and I galloped them about up and down the fields and all about the orchard for a good hour. They had each cut a great hazel stick for a riding-whip, and laid it on a little too hard, but I took it in good part, till at last I thought we had had enough, so I stopped two or three times by way of a hint. *Boys, you see, think a horse or pony is like a steam engine or a thrashing machine,* and can go on as long and as fast as they please. They never think that a pony can get tired, or have any feelings. So, as the one who was whipping me could not understand, I just rose up on my hind legs and let him slip off behind—that was all. He mounted me again, and I did the same. Then the other

PLATE I *My mother and I* (Page 4)

PLATE 2 *In double harness* (Page 22)

PLATE 3 *It fell right across the road* (Page 51)

PLATE 4 *I never was cleaned so lightly and quickly as by that little old man* (Page 63)

boy got up, and as soon as he began to use his stick I laid him on the grass, and so on, till they were able to understand, that was all. They are not bad boys; they don't wish to be cruel. I like them very well, but you see I had to give them a lesson. When they brought me to James and told him, I think he was very angry to see such big sticks. He said they were only fit for drovers or gypsies, and not for young gentlemen."

"If I had been you," said Ginger, "I would have given those boys a good kick, and that would have given them a lesson."

"No doubt you would," said Merrylegs, "but then I am not quite such a fool (begging your pardon) as to anger our master or make James ashamed of me; besides, those children are under my charge when they are riding. I tell you they are entrusted to me. Why, only the other day I heard our master say to Mrs. Bloomfield, 'My dear madam, you need not be anxious about the children; my old Merrylegs will take as much care of them as you or I could. I assure you I would not sell that pony for any money, he is so perfectly good-tempered and trustworthy.' And do you think I am such an ungrateful brute as to forget all the kind treatment I have had here for five years, and all the trust they place in me, and turn vicious because a couple of ignorant boys used me badly? No, No! You never had a good place where they were kind to you, and so you don't know, and I'm sorry for you; but I can tell you *good places make good horses.* I wouldn't vex our people for anything; I love them, I do," said Merrylegs, and he gave a low "ho, ho, ho," through his nose, as he used to do in the morning when he heard James's footstep at the door.

"Besides," he went on, "if I took to kicking, where should I be? Why, sold off in a jiffy, and no character, and I might find myself slaved about under a butcher's boy, or worked to death at some seaside place where no one cared for me, except to find out how fast I could go, or be flogged along in some cart with three or four great men in it going out for a Sunday spree, as I have often seen in the place I lived in before I came here. No," said he, shaking his head, "I hope I shall never come to that."

CHAPTER X

A Talk in the Orchard

GINGER AND I WERE NOT OF THE REGULAR TALL carriage-horse breed, we had more of the racing blood in us. We stood about fifteen and a half hands high; we were, therefore, just as good for riding as we were for driving, and our master used to say that he disliked either horse or man that could do but one thing. And, as he did not want to show off in London parks, he preferred a more active and useful kind of horse. As for us, our greatest pleasure was when we were saddled for a riding party, the master on Ginger, the mistress on me, and the young ladies on Sir Oliver and Merrylegs. It was so cheerful to be trotting and cantering all together that it always put us in high spirits. I had the best of it, for I always carried the mistress. Her weight was little, her voice was sweet, and her hand was so light on the rein that I was guided almost without feeling it.

Oh! If people knew what a comfort to horses a light hand is, and how it keeps a good mouth and a good temper, they surely would not chuck and drag and pull at the rein as they often do. Our mouths are so tender, that where they have not been spoiled or hardened with bad or ignorant treatment they feel the slightest movement of the driver's hand, and we know in an instant what is required of us. My mouth had never been spoiled, and I believe that was why the mistress preferred me to Ginger, although her paces were certainly quite as good. She used often to envy me, and said it was all the fault of breaking in, and the gag bit in London, that her mouth was not so perfect as mine. And then old Sir Oliver would say, "There, there! Don't vex yourself; you have the greatest honor. A mare that can carry a tall man of our master's weight, with all your spring and sprightly action, does not need to hold her head down because she does not carry the lady. We horses must take things as they come, and always be contented and willing so long as we are kindly used."

I had often wondered how it was that Sir Oliver had such a very short tail; it really was only six or seven inches long, with a tassel of hair hanging from it, and on one of our holidays in the orchard I ventured to ask him by what accident it was that he had lost his tail.

"Accident!" he snorted with a fierce look. "It was no accident! *It was a cruel, shameful, cold-blooded act!* When I was young I was taken to a place where these cruel things were done. I was tied up and made fast so that I could not stir, and then they came and cut off my long, beautiful tail, through the flesh and through the bone, and took it away."

"How dreadful!" I exclaimed.

"Dreadful! Ah, it was dreadful! But it was not only the pain, though that was terrible and lasted a long time; it was not only the indignity of having my best ornament taken from me, though that was bad, but it was this: *how could I ever brush the flies off my sides and my hind legs any more?* You who have tails just whisk the flies without thinking about it, and you can't tell what a torment it is to have them settle upon you and sting and sting, and have nothing in the world to lash them off with. I tell you it is a life-long wrong and a life-long loss. But thank Heaven, they don't do it now!"

"What did they do it for, then?" said Ginger.

"For fashion!" said the old horse with a stamp of his foot. "*For fashion!* if you know what that means. There was not a well-bred young horse in my time that had not his tail docked in that shameful way, just *as if the good God that made us did not know what he wanted, and what looked best.*"

"I suppose it is fashion that makes them strap our heads up with those horrid bits that I was tortured with in London," said Ginger.

"Of course it is," said he. "To my mind fashion is one of the wickedest things in the world. Now look, for instance, at the way they serve dogs, cutting off their tails to make them look plucky, and shearing up their pretty little ears to a point to make them look sharp, forsooth. I had a dear friend once, a brown terrier, 'Skye,' they called her. She was so fond of me that she never would sleep out of my stall. She made her bed under the manger, and there she had a litter of five, as pretty little puppies as need be. None were drowned, for they were a valuable kind, and how pleased she was with them! And when they got their eyes open and crawled about, it was a real pretty sight. But one day the man came and took them all away. I thought he might be afraid I should tread upon them. But it was not so. In the evening poor Skye brought them back again, one by one, in her mouth; not the happy little things that they were, but bleeding and crying pitifully. They had all had a piece of their tails cut off, and the soft flap of their pretty little ears was cut quite off. How their mother licked them, and how troubled she was, poor thing! I never forgot it. They healed in time, and they forgot the pain, but the nice soft flap, that of course was *intended to protect the delicate part of their ears from dust and injury, was gone forever. Why don't they cut their own children's ears into points to make them look sharp?* Why don't they cut the end off their noses to make them look plucky? One would be just as sensible as the other. What right have they to torment and disfigure God's creatures?"

Sir Oliver, though he was so gentle, was a fiery old fellow, and what he said was all so new to me and so dreadful, that I found a bitter feeling toward men rise up in my mind that I had never had before. Of course Ginger was much excited; she flung up her head with flashing eyes and distended nostrils, declaring that men were both brutes and blockheads.

"Who talks about blockheads?" said Merrylegs, who had just come up from the old apple-tree, where he had been rubbing himself against the low branch. "Who talks about blockheads? I believe that is a bad word."

"Bad words were made for bad things," said Ginger, and she told him what Sir Oliver had said.

"It is all true," said Merrylegs, sadly, "and I've seen that about the dogs over and over again where I lived first; but we won't talk about it here. You know that master and John and James are always good to us, and talking against men in such a place as this doesn't seem fair or grateful, and you know there are good masters and good grooms besides ours, though of course ours are the best."

This wise speech of good little Merrylegs, which we knew was quite true, cooled us all down, especially Sir Oliver, who was dearly fond of his master. And to turn the subject I said, "Can anyone tell me the use of blinkers?"

"No!" said Sir Oliver, shortly, "because they are no use."

"They are supposed," said Justice, the roan cob, in his calm way, "to prevent horses from shying and starting, and getting so frightened as to cause accidents."

"Then what is the reason they do not put them on riding horses, especially on ladies' horses?" said I.

"There is no reason at all," said he quietly, "except *the fashion.* They say that a horse would be so frightened to see the wheels of his own cart or carriage coming behind him that he would be sure to run away, although of course when he is ridden, he sees them all about him if the streets are crowded. I admit they do sometimes come too close to be pleasant, but we don't run away; we are used to it and understand it, and if we never had blinkers put on we should never want them. We should see what was there, and know what was what, and be much less frightened than by only seeing bits of things that we can't understand. Of course there may be some nervous horses who have been hurt or frightened when they were young, and may be the better for them; but as I never was nervous, I can't judge."

"I consider," said Sir Oliver, "*that blinkers are dangerous things in the night.* We horses can see much better in the dark than men can, and many an accident would never have happened if horses might have had the full use of their eyes. Some years ago, I remember, there was a hearse with two horses returning one dark night, and just by Farmer Sparrow's house, where the pond is close to the road, the wheels went too near the edge, and the hearse was overturned into the water. Both the horses were drowned, and the driver hardly escaped. Of course after this accident a stout white rail was put up that might be easily seen; *but if those horses had not been partly blinded,* they would of themselves have kept farther from the edge, and no accident would have happened.

"When our master's carriage was overturned, before you came here, it was said that if the lamp on the left side had not gone out, John would have seen the great hole that the road-makers had left. And so he might, *but if old Colin had not had blinkers on* he would have seen it, lamp or no lamp, for he was far too knowing an old horse to run into danger. As it was, he was very much hurt, the carriage was broken, and how John escaped nobody knew."

"I should say," said Ginger, curling her nostril, "that these men, who are so wise, had better give orders that in future all foals should be born with their eyes set just in the middle of their foreheads, instead of on the side. They always think they can improve upon Nature and mend what God has made."

Things were getting rather sore again, when Merrylegs held up his knowing little face and said, "I'll tell you a secret: I believe John does not approve of blinkers. I heard him talking with master about it one day. The master said that 'if horses had been used to them, it might be dangerous in some cases to leave them off,' and John said *he thought it would be a good thing if all colts were broken in without blinkers, as was the case in some foreign countries.*

So, let us cheer up, and have a run to the other end of the orchard; I believe the wind has blown down some apples, we might just as well eat them as the slugs."

Merrylegs could not be resisted, so we broke off our long conversation and got up our spirits by munching some very sweet apples which lay scattered on the grass.

CHAPTER XI

Plain Speaking

THE LONGER I LIVED AT BIRTWICK, THE MORE proud and happy I felt at having such a place. Our master and mistress were respected and beloved by all who knew them. They were good and kind to everybody and everything—not only men and women, but horses and donkeys, dogs and cats, cattle and birds. There was no oppressed or ill-used creature that had not a friend in them, and their servants took the same tone. If any of the village children were known to treat any creature cruelly, they soon heard about it from the Hall.

The Squire and Farmer Grey had worked together, as they said, for more than twenty years, to get check-reins on the cart-horses done away with, and in our parts you seldom saw them. But sometimes, if mistress met a heavily laden horse with his head strained up, she would stop the carriage and get out, and reason with the driver in her sweet serious voice, and try to show him how foolish and cruel it was.

I don't think any man could withstand our mistress. I wish all ladies were like her. Our master, too, used to come down very heavy sometimes. I remember he was riding me toward home one morning, when we saw a powerful man driving toward us in a light pony chaise, with a beautiful little bay pony with slender legs and a high-bred, sensitive head and face. Just as he came to the Park gates, the little thing turned toward them. The man, without word or warning, wrenched the creature's head around with such force and suddenness that he nearly threw it on its haunches. Recovering itself, it was going on when he began to lash it furiously. The pony plunged forward, but the strong, heavy hand held the pretty creature back with force almost enough to break its jaw, while the whip still cut into him. It was a dreadful sight to me, for I knew what fearful pain it gave that delicate little mouth; but master gave me the word, and we were up with him in a second.

"Sawyer," he cried in a stern voice, "is that pony made of flesh and blood?"

"Flesh and blood and temper," he said. "He's too fond of his own will, and that won't suit me." He spoke as if he was in a strong passion. He was a builder, who had often been to the Park on business.

"And do you think," said master sternly, "that treatment like this will make him fond of your will?"

"He had no business to make that turn; his road was straight on!" said the man roughly.

"You have often driven that pony up to my place," said master. "It only shows the creature's memory and intelligence. How did he know that you were not going there again? But that has little to do with it. I must say, Mr. Sawyer, that more unmanly, brutal treatment of a little pony it was never my painful lot to witness; and by giving way to such passion you injure your own character as much—nay, more—than you injure your horse, and remember, we shall all have to be judged according to our works, whether they be toward man or toward beast."

Master rode me home slowly, and I could tell by his voice how the thing had grieved him. He was just as free to speak to gentlemen of his own rank as to those below him, for another day, when we were out, we met a Captain Langley, a friend of our master; he was driving a splendid pair of grays in a kind of break. After a little conversation the Captain said:

"What do you think of my new team, Mr. Douglas? You know you are the judge of horses in these parts, and I should like your opinion."

The master backed me a little, so as to get a good view of them. "They are an uncommonly handsome pair," he said, "and if they are as good as they look, I am sure you need not wish for anything better. But I see you still hold that pet scheme of yours for worrying your horses and lessening their power."

"What do you mean," said the other, "the check-reins? Oh, ah! I know that's a hobby of yours. Well, the fact is, I like to see my horses hold their heads up."

"So do I," said master, "as well as any man, but I don't like to see them *held up;* that takes all the shine out of it. Now, you are a military man, Langley, and no doubt like to see your regiment look well on parade—'Heads up,' and all that—but you would not take much credit for your drill if all your men had their heads tied to a back-board! It might not be much harm on parade, except to worry and fatigue them; *but how would it be in a bayonet charge against the enemy,* when they want the free use of every muscle, and all their strength thrown forward? I would not give much for your chance of victory. And it is just the same with horses: *you fret and worry their tempers and decrease their power;* you will not let them throw their weight against their work, and so they have to do too much with their joints and muscles, and of course it wears them up faster. You may depend upon it, horses were intended to have their heads free, as free as men's are; and if we would act a little more according to common sense, and a good deal less according to fashion, we should find many things work easier. Besides, you know as well as I that if a horse makes a false step, he has *much less chance of recovering himself if his head and neck are fastened back.* And now," said the master, laughing, "I have given my hobby a good trot out. Can't you make up your mind to mount him, too, Captain? Your example would go a long way."

"I believe you are right in theory," said the other, "and that's rather a hard bit about the soldiers; but—well—I'll think about it," and so they parted.

CHAPTER XII

A Stormy Day

ONE DAY LATE IN THE AUTUMN MY MASTER HAD A long journey to go on business. I was put into the dog-cart, and John went with his master. I always liked to go in the dog-cart, it was so light, and the high wheels ran along so pleasantly. There had been a great deal of rain, and now the wind was very high and blew the dry leaves across the road in a shower. We went along merrily till we came to the toll bar and the low wooden bridge. The river banks were rather high, and the bridge, instead of rising, went across just level, so that in the middle, if the river was full, the water would be nearly up to the woodwork and planks. But as there were good substantial rails on each side, people did not mind it.

The man at the gate said the river was rising fast, and he feared it would be a bad night. Many of the meadows were under water, and in one low part of the road, the water was halfway up to my knees. The bottom was good, and master drove gently, so it was no matter.

When we got to the town, of course I had a good wait, but as the master's business engaged him a long time, we did not start for home till rather late in the afternoon. The wind was then much higher, and I heard the master say to John, he had never been out in such a storm; and so I thought, as we went along the skirts of a wood, where the great branches were swaying about like twigs, and the rushing sound was terrible.

"I wish we were well out of this wood," said my master.

"Yes, sir," said John, "it would be rather awkward if one of these branches came down upon us."

The words were scarcely out of his mouth when there was a groan, and a crack, and a splitting sound; and tearing, crashing down among the other trees came an oak, torn up by the roots, and it fell right across the road just before us. I will never say I was not frightened, for I was. I stopped still, and I believe I trembled. Of course I did not turn round or run away; I was not brought up to that. John jumped out and was in a moment at my head.

"That was a very near touch," said my master. "What's to be done now?"

"Well, sir, we can't drive over that tree nor yet get round it. There will be nothing for it but to go back to the four crossways, and that will be a good six miles before we get round to the wooden bridge again. It will make us late, but the horse is fresh."

So back we went and round by the crossroads, but by the time we got to the bridge it was very nearly dark. We could just see that the water was over the middle of it, but as that happened sometimes when the floods were out, master did not stop. We were going along at a good pace, but the moment my feet touched *the first part of the bridge I felt sure there was something wrong.* I dared not go forward, and I made a dead stop. "Go on, Beauty," said my master, and he gave me a touch with the whip, but I dared not stir. He gave me a sharp cut; I jumped, but I dared not go forward.

"There's something wrong, sir," said John, and he sprang out of the dog-cart, and came to my head and looked all about. He tried to lead me forward. "Come on, Beauty, what's the matter?" Of course I could not tell him, but I knew very well that the bridge was not safe.

Just then the man at the toll-gate on the other side ran out of the house, tossing a torch about like one mad.

"Hoy, hoy, hoy! Halloo! Stop!" he cried.

"What's the matter?" shouted my master.

"The bridge is broken in the middle, and part of it is carried away. If you come on, you'll be into the river."

"Thank God!" said my master.

"You Beauty!" said John, and took the bridle and gently turned me round to the right-hand road by the river side. The sun had set some time ago, the wind seemed to have lulled off after that furious blast which tore up the tree. It grew darker and darker, stiller and stiller. I trotted quietly along, the wheels hardly making a sound on the soft road. For a good while neither master nor John spoke, and then master began in a serious voice. I could not understand much of what they said, but I found they thought, if I had gone on as the master wanted me, most likely the bridge would have given way under us, and horse, chaise, master, and man would have fallen into the river. And as the current was flowing very strongly, and there was no light and no help at hand, it was more than likely we should all have been drowned.

Master said God had given men reason, by which they could find out things for themselves; but He had given animals knowledge, which did not depend on reason, and which was much more prompt and perfect in its way, and by which they had often saved the lives of men. John had many stories to tell of dogs and horses, and the wonderful things they had done. He thought people did not value their animals half enough, nor make friends of them as they ought to do. I am sure he makes friends of them, if ever a man did.

At last we came to the park gates and found the gardener looking out for us. He said that mistress had been in a dreadful way ever since dark, fearing some accident had happened, and that she had sent James off on Justice, the roan cob, toward the wooden bridge to make inquiry after us.

We saw a light at the hall door and at the upper windows, and as we came up mistress ran out, saying, "Are you really safe, my dear? Oh! I have been so anxious, fancying all sorts of things. Have you had no accident?"

"No, my dear, but if your Black Beauty had not been wiser than we were, we should all have been carried down the river at the wooden bridge." I heard no more, as they went into the house and John took me to the stable. Oh, what a good supper he gave me that night, a good bran mash and some crushed beans with my oats, and such a thick bed of straw! And I was glad of it, for I was tired.

CHAPTER XIII

The Devil's Trademark

ONE DAY WHEN JOHN AND I HAD BEEN OUT ON some business of my master's and were returning gently on a long, straight road, at some distance we saw a boy trying to leap a pony over a gate. The pony would not take the leap, and the boy cut him with the whip, but he only turned off on one side. He whipped him again, but the pony turned off on the other side. Then the boy got off and gave him a hard thrashing and knocked him about the head; then he got up again and tried to make him leap the gate, kicking him all the time shamefully, but still the pony refused. When we were nearly at the spot, the pony put down his head and threw up his heels and sent the boy neatly over into a broad quickset hedge, and with the rein dangling from his head, he set off home at a full gallop. John laughed out quite loud. "Served him right," he said.

"Oh! oh! oh!" cried the boy as he struggled about amongst the thorns. "I say, come and help me out."

"Thank ye," said John, "I think you are quite in the right place, and maybe a little scratching will teach you not to leap a pony over a gate that is too high for him." And so with that John rode off. "It may be," said he to himself, "that young fellow is a liar as well as a cruel one. We'll just go home by Farmer Bushby's, Beauty, and then if anybody wants to know, you and I can tell 'em, ye see." So we turned off to the right and soon came up to the stack-yard, and within sight of the house. The farmer was hurrying out into the road, and his wife was standing at the gate, looking very frightened.

"Have you seen my boy?" said Mr. Bushby as we came up. "He went out an hour ago on my black pony, and the creature is just come back without a rider."

"I should think, sir," said John, "he had better be without a rider, unless he can be ridden properly."

"What do you mean?" said the farmer.

"Well, sir, I saw your son whipping, and kicking, and knocking that good little pony about shamefully because he would not leap a gate that was too high for him. The pony behaved well, sir, and showed no vice, but at last he just threw up his heels and tipped the young gentleman into the thorn hedge. He wanted me to help him out; but I hope you will excuse me, sir, I did not feel inclined to do so. There's no bones broken, sir, he'll only get a few scratches. I love horses, and it riles me to see them badly used. It is a bad plan to aggravate an animal till he uses his heels; the first time is not always the last."

During this time the mother began to cry, "Oh, my poor Bill! I must go and meet him; he must be hurt."

"You had better go into the house, wife," said the farmer. "Bill wants a lesson about this, and I must see that he gets it. This is not the first time, nor the second, that he has ill-used that pony, and I shall stop it. I am much obliged to you, Manly. Good evening."

So we went on, John chuckling all the way home. Then he told James about it, who laughed and said, "Served him right. I knew that boy at school. He took great airs on himself because he was a farmer's son; he used to swagger about and bully the little boys. Of course we elder ones would not have any of that nonsense, and let him know that in the school and the playground, farmers' sons and laborers' sons were all alike. I well remember one day, just before afternoon school, I found him at the large window catching flies and pulling off their wings. He did not see me, and I gave him a box on the ears that laid him sprawling on the floor. Well, angry as I was, I was almost frightened, he roared and bellowed in such a style. The boys rushed in from the playground and the master ran in from the road to see who was being murdered. Of course, I said fair and square at once what I had done, and why; then I showed the master the poor flies, some crushed and some crawling about helpless, and I showed him the wings on the windowsill. I never saw him so angry before. But as Bill was still howling and whining, like the coward that he was, he did not give him any more punishment of that kind, but set him up on a stool for the rest of the afternoon, and said that he should not go out to play for that week. Then he talked to all the boys very seriously about cruelty, and said how hard-hearted and cowardly it was to hurt the weak and the helpless. But what stuck in my mind was this: he said that *cruelty was the devil's own trademark,* and if we saw anyone who took pleasure in cruelty, we might know who he belonged to, for the devil was a murderer from the beginning, and a tormentor to the end. On the other hand, where we saw people who loved their neighbors, and were kind to man and beast, we might know that was God's mark, for 'God is Love.' "

"Your master never taught you a truer thing," said John. "There is no religion without love, and people may talk as much as they like about their religion, but *if it does not teach them to be good and kind to man and beast, it is all a sham*—all a sham, James, and it won't stand when things come to be turned inside out and put down for what they are."

CHAPTER XIV

James Howard

ONE MORNING EARLY IN DECEMBER JOHN HAD just led me into my box after my daily exercise, and was strapping my cloth on, and James was coming in from the corn chamber with some oats, when the master came into the stable. He looked rather serious, and held an open letter in his hand. John fastened the door of my box, touched his cap, and waited for orders.

"Good morning, John," said the master. "I want to know if you have any complaint to make of James?"

"Complaint, sir? No, sir."

"Is he industrious at work and respectful to you?"

"Yes, sir, always."

"You never find he slights his work when your back is turned?"

"Never, sir."

"That's well; but I must put another question: have you any reason to suspect that when he goes out with the horses to exercise them, or to take a message, he stops about, talking to his acquaintances, or goes into houses where he has no business, leaving the horses outside?"

"No, sir, certainly not, and if anybody has been saying that about James, I don't believe it, and I don't mean to believe it unless I have it fairly proved before witnesses. It's not for me to say who has been trying to take away James's character, but I will say this, sir, that a steadier, pleasanter, honester, smarter young fellow I never had in this stable. I can trust his word and I can trust his work; he is gentle and clever with the horses, and I would rather have them in his charge than in that of half the young fellows I know in laced hats and liveries. And whoever wants a character of James Howard," said John, with a decided jerk of his head, "let them come to John Manly."

The master stood all this time grave and attentive, but as John finished his speech a broad smile spread over his face, and looking kindly across at James, who all this time had stood still at the door, he said, "James, my lad, set down the oats and come here. I am very glad to find that John's opinion of your character agrees so exactly with my own. John is a cautious man," he said, with a droll smile, "and it is not always easy to get his opinion about people, so I thought if I beat the bush on this side the birds would fly out, and I should learn what I wanted to know quickly. So now we will come to business. I have a letter from my brother-in-law, Sir Clifford Williams, of Clifford Hall. He wants me to find him a trustworthy young groom, about twenty or twenty-one, who knows his business. His old coachman, who has lived with him thirty years, is getting feeble, and he wants a man to work with him and get into his ways who would be able, when the old man was pensioned off, to step into his place. He would have eighteen shillings a week at first, a stable suit, a driving suit, a bedroom over the coach-house, and a boy under him. Sir Clifford is a good master, and if you could get the place, it would be a good start for you. I don't want to part with you, and if you left us I know John would lose his right hand."

"That I should, sir," said John, "but I would not stand in his light for the world."

"How old are you, James?" said master.

"Nineteen next May, sir."

"That's young. What do you think, John?"

"Well, sir, it is young, but he is as steady as a man, and is strong, and well grown, and though he has not had much experience in driving, he has a light, firm hand and a quick eye, and he is very careful, and I am quite sure no horse of his will be ruined for want of having his feet and shoes looked after."

"Your word will go the furthest, John," said the master, "for Sir Clifford adds in a postscript, 'If I could find a man trained by your John, I should like him better than any other.' So, James, lad, think it over, talk to your mother at dinnertime, and then let me know what you wish."

In a few days after this conversation it was fully settled that James should go to Clifford Hall in a month or six weeks, as it suited his master, and in the meantime he was to get all the practice in driving that could be given to him. I never knew the carriage to go out so often before. When the mistress did not go out, the master drove himself in the two-wheeled chaise; but now, whether it was master or the young ladies, or only an errand, Ginger and I were put into the carriage and James drove us. At the first John rode with him on the box, telling him this and that, and after that James drove alone.

Then it was wonderful what a number of places the master would go to in the city on Saturday, and what queer streets we were driven through. He was sure to go to the railway station just as the train was coming in, and cabs and carriages, carts and omnibuses, were all trying to get over the bridge together. That bridge wanted good horses and good drivers when the railway bell was ringing, for it was narrow, and there was a very sharp turn up to the station, where it would not have been at all difficult for people to run into each other if they did not look sharp.

CHAPTER XV

The Old Ostler

AFTER THIS, IT WAS DECIDED BY MY MASTER AND mistress to pay a visit to some friends who lived about forty-six miles from our home, and James was to drive them. The first day we traveled thirty-two miles. There were some long, heavy hills, but James drove so carefully and thoughtfully that we were not at all harassed. He never forgot to put on the brake as we went downhill, nor to take it off at the right place. He kept our feet on the smoothest part of the road, and if the uphill was very long, he set the carriage wheels a little across the road, so as not to run back, and gave us a breathing. All these little things help a horse very much, *particularly if he gets kind words into the bargain.*

We stopped once or twice on the road, and just as the sun was going down we reached the town where we were to spend the night. We stopped at the principal hotel, which was in the marketplace. It was a very large one. We drove under an archway into a long yard, at the further end of which were the stables and coach-houses. Two ostlers came to take us out. The head ostler was a pleasant, active little man, with a crooked leg and a yellow striped waistcoat. I never saw a man unbuckle harness so quickly as he did, and with a pat and a good word he led me to a long stable, with six or eight stalls in it and two or three horses. The other man brought Ginger. James stood by while we were rubbed down and cleaned.

I never was cleaned so lightly and quickly as by that little old man. When he had done, James stepped up and felt me over, as if he thought I could not be thoroughly done, but he found my coat as clean and smooth as silk.

"Well," he said, "I thought I was pretty quick, and our John quicker still, but you do beat all I ever saw for being quick and thorough at the same time."

"Practice makes perfect," said the crooked little ostler, "and 'twould be a pity if it didn't; forty years' practice, and not perfect! Ha, ha! That would be a pity. And as to being quick, why bless you! that is only a matter of habit. If you get into the habit of being quick, it is just as easy as being slow; easier, I should say; in fact, it don't agree with my health to be hulking about over a job twice as long as it need take. Bless you! I couldn't whistle if I crawled over my work as some folks do!

"You see, I have been about horses ever since I was twelve years old, in hunting stables and racing stables. And being small, ye see, I was a jockey for several years. But at the Goodwood, ye see, the turf was very slippery and my poor Larkspur got a fall, and I broke my knee, and so, of course, I was of no more use there. But I could not live without horses, of course I couldn't, so I took to the hotels. And I can tell ye it is a downright pleasure to handle an animal like this, well-bred, well-mannered, well-cared for, bless ye! *I can tell how a horse is treated. Give me the handling of a horse for twenty minutes, and I'll tell you what sort of a groom he has had.* Look at this one, pleasant, quiet, turns about just as you want him, holds up his feet to be cleaned out, or anything else you please to wish. Then you'll find another, fidgety, fretty, won't move the right way, or starts across the stall, tosses up his head as soon as you come near him, lays his ears, and seems afraid of you, or else squares about at you with his heels. Poor things! I know what sort of treatment they have had. If they are timid, it makes them start or shy; if they are high-mettled, it makes them vicious or dangerous. Their tempers are mostly made when they are young. Bless you! *They are like children; train 'em up in the way they should go, as the good book says, and when they are old they will not depart from it,* if they have a chance, that is."

"I like to hear you talk," said James. "That's the way we lay it down at home, at our master's."

"Who is your master, young man? If it be a proper question. I should judge he is a good one, from what I see."

"He is Squire Gordon, of Birtwick Park, the other side the Beacon Hills," said James.

"Ah! So, so, I have heard tell of him. Fine judge of horses, ain't he? The best rider in the county?"

"I believe he is," said James, "but he rides very little now, since the poor young master was killed."

"Ah, poor gentleman! I read all about it in the paper at the time. A fine horse killed too, wasn't there?"

"Yes," said James, "he was a splendid creature, brother to this one, and just like him."

"Pity, pity!" said the old man. " 'Twas a bad place to leap, if I remember—a thin fence at top, a steep bank down to the stream, wasn't it? No chance for a horse to see where he is going. Now, I am for bold riding as much as any man, but still there are some leaps that only a very knowing old huntsman has any right to take. *A man's life and a horse's life are worth more than a fox's tail,* at least I should say they ought to be."

During this time the other man had finished Ginger, and had brought our corn, and James and the old man left the stable together.

CHAPTER XVI

The Fire

LATER ON IN THE EVENING A TRAVELER'S HORSE was brought in by the second ostler, and while he was cleaning him a young man with a pipe in his mouth lounged into the stable to gossip.

"I say, Towler," said the ostler, "just run up the ladder into the loft and put some hay down into this horse's rack, will you? *Only, lay down your pipe.*"

"All right," said the other, and went up through the trap door, and I heard him step across the floor overhead and put down the hay. James came in to look at us the last thing, and then the door was locked.

I cannot say how long I had slept, nor what time in the night it was, but I woke up very uncomfortable, though I hardly knew why. I got up, the air seemed all thick and choking. I heard Ginger coughing, and one of the other horses seemed very restless. It was quite dark, and I could see nothing, but the stable seemed full of smoke and I hardly knew how to breathe.

The trap door had been left open, and I thought that was the place it came through. I listened and heard a soft rushing sort of noise, and a low crackling and snapping. I did not know what it was, but there was something in the sound so strange that it made me tremble all over. The other horses were now all awake; some were pulling at their halters, others were stamping.

At last I heard steps outside, and the ostler who had put up the traveler's horse burst into the stable with a lantern, and began to untie the horses and try to lead them out. But he seemed in such a hurry and so frightened himself that he frightened me still more. The first horse would not go with him; he tried the second and third, and they, too, would not stir. He came to me next and tried to drag me out of the stall by force; of course that was no use. He tried us all by turns and then left the stable.

No doubt we were very foolish, but danger seemed to be all around, and there was nobody we knew to trust in, and all was strange and uncertain. The fresh air that had come in through the open door made it easier to breathe, but the rushing sound overhead grew louder, and as I looked upward through the bars of my empty rack I saw a red light flickering on the wall. Then I heard a cry of "Fire!" outside, and the old ostler quietly and quickly came in. He got one horse out and went to another, but the flames were playing round the trap-door, and the roaring overhead was dreadful.

The next thing I heard was James's voice, quiet and cheery, as it always was.

"Come, my beauties, it is time for us to be off, so wake up and come along." I stood nearest the door, so he came to me first, patting me as he came in.

"Come, Beauty, on with your bridle, my boy, we will soon be out of this smother." It was on in no time, then he took the scarf off his neck and tied it lightly over my eyes, and patting and coaxing, he led me out of the stable. Safe in the yard, he slipped the scarf off my eyes and shouted, "Here, somebody! Take this horse while I go back for the other."

A tall, broad man stepped forward and took me, and James darted back into the stable. I set up a shrill whinny as I saw him go. Ginger told me afterward that whinny was the best thing I could have done for her, for had she not heard me outside, she would never have had courage to come out.

There was much confusion in the yard, the horses being got out of other stables, and the carriages and gigs being pulled out of houses and sheds, lest the flames should spread further. On the other side of the yard, windows were thrown up, and people were shouting all sorts of things; but I kept my eye fixed on the stable door, where the smoke poured out thicker than ever, and I could see flashes of red light. Presently I heard above all the stir and din a loud, clear voice, which I knew was master's:

"James Howard! James Howard! Are you there?"

There was no answer, but I heard a crash of something falling in the stable, and the next moment I gave a loud, joyful neigh, for I saw James coming through the smoke, leading Ginger with him. She was coughing violently, and he was not able to speak.

"My brave lad!" said master, laying his hand on his shoulder. "Are you hurt?"

James shook his head, for he could not yet speak.

"Aye," said the big man who held me, "he is a brave lad, and no mistake."

"And now," said master, "when you have got your breath, James, we'll get out of this place as quickly as we can." And we were moving toward the entry, when from the marketplace there came a sound of galloping feet and loud rumbling wheels.

" 'Tis the fire engine! the fire engine!" shouted two or three voices. "Stand back, make way!" And clattering and thundering over the stones, two horses dashed into the yard with the heavy engine behind them. The fireman leaped to the ground. There was no need to ask where the fire was—it was torching up in a great blaze from the roof.

We got out as fast as we could into the broad, quiet marketplace. The stars were shining, and except the noise behind us, all was still. Master led the way to a large hotel on the other side, and as soon as the ostler came, he said, "James, I must now hasten to your mistress. I trust the horses entirely to you; order whatever you think is needed." And with that he was gone. The master did not run, but I never saw mortal man walk so fast as he did that night.

There was a dreadful sound before we got into our stalls: the shrieks of those poor horses that were left burning to death in the stable—it was very terrible and made both Ginger and me feel very bad. We, however, were taken in and well done by.

The next morning the master came to see how we were and to speak to James. I did not hear much, for the ostler was rubbing me down, but I could see that James looked very happy, and I thought the master was proud of him. Our mistress had been so much alarmed in the night that the journey was put off till the afternoon, so James had the morning on hand, and went first to the inn to see about our harness and the carriage, and then to hear more about the fire. When he came back, we heard him tell the ostler about it. At first no one could guess how the fire had been caused, but at last a man said he *saw Dick Towler go into the stable with a pipe in his mouth,* and when he came out he had not one and went to the tap for another. Then the under ostler said he had asked Dick to go up the ladder to put down some hay, but told him to lay down his pipe first. Dick denied taking the pipe with him, but no one believed him. I remember our John Manly's rule, *never to allow a pipe in the stable,* and thought it ought to be the rule everywhere.

James said the roof and floor had all fallen in, and only the black walls were standing. The two poor horses that could not be got out were buried under the burned rafters and tiles.

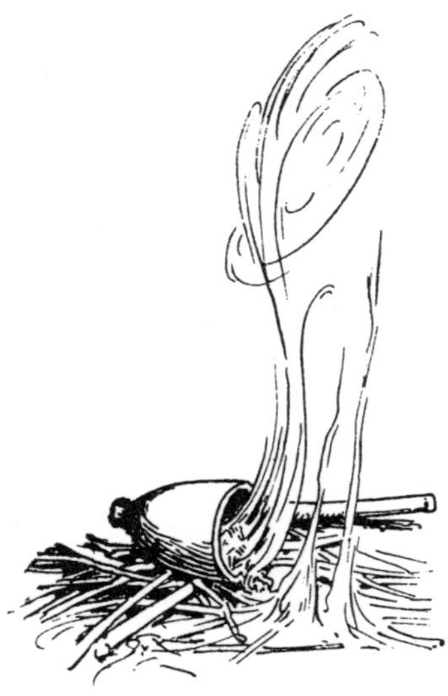

CHAPTER XVII

John Manly's Talk

THE REST OF OUR JOURNEY WAS VERY EASY, AND a little after sunset we reached the house of my master's friend. We were taken into a clean, snug stable. There was a kind coachman, who made us very comfortable, and who seemed to think a good deal of James when he heard about the fire.

"There is one thing quite clear, young man," he said, "your horses know who they can trust. It is one of the hardest things in the world to get horses out of a stable when there is either fire or flood. I don't know why they won't come out, but they won't—not one in twenty."

We stopped two or three days at this place and then returned home. All went well on the journey. We were glad to be in our own stable again, and John was equally glad to see us.

Before he and James left us for the night, James said, "I wonder who is coming in my place."

"Little Joe Green at the Lodge," said John.

"Little Joe Green! Why, he's a child!"

"He's fourteen and a half," said John.

"But he is such a little chap!"

"Yes, he is small, but he is quick, and willing, and kind-hearted, too, and then he wishes very much to come, and his father would like it, and I know the master would like to give him the chance. He said if I thought he would not do, he would look out for a bigger boy, but I said I was quite agreeable to try him for six weeks."

"Six weeks!" said James. "Why, it will be six months before he can be of much use! It will make you a deal of work, John."

"Well," said John with a laugh, "work and I are very good friends. I never was afraid of work yet."

"You are a very good man," said James. "I wish I may ever be like you."

"I don't often speak of myself," said John, "but as you are going away from us out into the world, to shift for yourself, I'll just tell you how I look on these things. I was just as old as Joseph when my father and mother died of the fever, within ten days of each other, and left me and my crippled sister Nelly alone in the world, without a relation that we could look to for help. I was a farmer's boy, not earning enough to keep myself, much less both of us, and she must have gone to the workhouse but for our mistress (Nelly calls her her angel, and she has good right to do so). She went and hired a room for her with old Widow Mallet, and she gave her knitting and needlework when she was able to do it. And when she was ill, she sent her dinners and many nice, comfortable things, and was like a mother to her. Then the master, he took me into the stable under old

Norman, the coachman that was then. I had my food at the house, and my bed in the loft, and a suit of clothes and three shillings a week, so that I could help Nelly.

"Then there was Norman. He might have turned round and said that at his age he could not be troubled with a raw boy from the plow-tail, but he was like a father to me, and took no end of pains with me. When the old man died some years after, I stepped into his place, and now of course I have top wages and can lay by for a rainy day or a sunny day, as it may happen, and Nelly is as happy as a bird. So you see, James, I am not the man that should turn up his nose at a little boy and vex a good, kind master. No, no! I shall miss you very much, James, but we shall pull through, and *there's nothing like doing a kindness when 'tis put in your way, and I am glad I can do it.*"

"Then," said James, "you don't hold with that saying, 'Everybody look after himself and take care of number one.' "

"No, indeed," said John. "Where should I and Nelly have been if master and mistress and old Norman had only taken care of number one? Why, she in the workhouse and I hoeing turnips! Where would Black Beauty and Ginger have been if you had only thought of number one? Why, roasted to death! No, Jim, no! That is a selfish, heathenish saying, whoever uses it; and any man who thinks he has nothing to do but take care of number one, why, it's a pity but what he had been drowned like a puppy or a kitten before he got his eyes open—that's what I think," said John, with a very decided jerk of his head.

James laughed at this, but there was a thickness in his voice when he said, "You have been my best friend except my mother. I hope you won't forget me."

"No, lad, no!" said John. "And if ever I can do you a good turn I hope you won't forget me."

The next day Joe came to the stables to learn all he could before James left. He learned to sweep the stable and to bring in the straw and hay; he began to clean the harness and helped to wash the carriage. As he was quite too short to do anything in the way of grooming Ginger and me, James taught him upon Merrylegs, for he was to have full charge of him, under John. He was a nice little bright fellow, and always came whistling to his work.

Merrylegs was a good deal put out at being "mauled about," as he said, "by a boy who knew nothing." But toward the end of the second week he told me confidentially that he thought the boy would turn out well.

At last the day came when James had to leave us. Cheerful as he always was, he looked quite down-hearted that morning.

"You see," he said to John, "I am leaving a great deal behind: my mother, and Betsy, and you, and a good master and mistress, and then the horses, and my old Merrylegs. At the new place there will not be a soul that I shall know. If it were not that I shall get a higher place and be able to help my mother better, I don't think I should have made up my mind to it; it is a real pinch, John."

"Aye, James, lad, so it is, but I should not think much of you if you could leave your home for the first time and not feel it. Cheer up, you'll make friends there, and if you get on well, as I am sure you will, it will be a fine thing for your mother, and she will be proud enough that you have got into such a good place as that."

So John cheered him up, but everyone was sorry to lose James. As for Merrylegs, he pined after him for several days and went quite off his appetite. So John took him out several mornings with a leading rein, when he exercised me, and trotting and galloping by my side got up the little fellow's spirits again, and he was soon all right.

Joe's father would often come in and give a little help, as he understood the work, and Joe took a great deal of pains to learn, and John was quite encouraged about him.

CHAPTER XVIII

Going for the Doctor

ONE NIGHT, A FEW DAYS AFTER JAMES HAD LEFT, I had eaten my hay and was lying down in my straw fast asleep, when I was suddenly roused by the stable-bell ringing very loud. I heard the door of John's house open, and his feet running up to the Hall. He was back again in no time. He unlocked the stable door and came in, calling out, "Wake up, Beauty, you must go well now, if ever you did." And almost before I could think, he had got the saddle on my back and the bridle on my head. He just ran round for his coat, and then took me at a quick trot up to the Hall door. The Squire stood there with a lamp in his hand.

"Now, John," he said, "ride for your life—that is, for your mistress's life. There is not a moment to lose. Give this note to Doctor White, give your horse a rest at the inn, and be back as soon as you can."

John said, "Yes, sir," and was on my back in a minute. The

gardener who lived at the lodge had heard the bell ring and was ready with the gate open, and away we went through the park, and through the village, and down the hill till we came to the toll-gate. John called very loud and thumped upon the door. The man was soon out and flung open the gate.

"Now," said John, "do you keep the gate open for the doctor; here's the money." And off we went again.

There was before us a long piece of level road by the riverside. John said to me, "Now, Beauty, do your best," And so I did. I wanted no whip nor spur, and for two miles I galloped as fast as I could lay my feet to the ground. I don't believe that my old grandfather, who won the race at Newmarket, could have gone faster. When we came to the bridge, John pulled me up a little and patted my neck. "Well done, Beauty, good old fellow!" he said. He would have let me go slower, but my spirit was up, and I was off again as fast as before. The air was frosty, the moon was bright, it was very pleasant. We came through a village, then through a dark wood, then uphill, then downhill, till after an eight-mile run we came to the town, through the streets, and into the marketplace. It was all quite still except the clatter of my feet on the stones—everybody was asleep. The church clock struck three as we drew up at Doctor White's door. John rang the bell twice, and then knocked at the door like thunder. A window was thrown up, and Doctor White, in his nightcap, put his head out and said, "What do you want?"

"Mrs. Gordon is very ill, sir; master wants you to go at once. He thinks she will die if you cannot get there. Here is a note."

"Wait," he said, "I will come."

He shut the window, and was soon at the door.

"The worst of it is," he said, "that my horse has been out all day and is quite done up; my son has just been sent for, and he has taken the other. What is to be done? Can I have your horse?"

"He has come at a gallop nearly all the way, sir, and I was to give him a rest here. But I think my master would not be against it if you think fit, sir."

"All right," he said, "I will soon be ready."

John stood by me and stroked my neck; I was very hot. The doctor came out with his riding-whip.

"You need not take that, sir," said John. "Black Beauty will go till he drops. Take care of him, sir, if you can. I should not like any harm to come to him."

"No, no, John!" said the doctor. "I hope not." And in a minute we had left John far behind.

I will not tell about our way back. The doctor was a heavier man than John, and not so good a rider; however, I did my very best. The man at the toll-gate had it open. When we came to the hill, the doctor drew me up. "Now, my good fellow," he said, "take some breath." I was glad he did, for I was nearly spent, but that breathing helped me on, and soon we were in the park. Joe was at the lodge gate. My master was at the Hall door, for he had heard us coming. He spoke not a word; the doctor went into the house with him, and Joe led me to the stable. I was glad to get home; my legs shook under me, and I could only stand and pant. I had not a dry hair on my body, the water ran down my legs, and I steamed all over—Joe used to say, like a pot on fire.

Poor Joe! He was young and small, and as yet he knew very little, and his father, who would have helped him, had been sent to the next village. But I am sure he did the very best he knew. He rubbed my legs and my chest, but he did not put my warm cloth on me. He thought I was so hot I should not like it. Then he gave me a pailful of water to drink. It was cold and very good, and I drank it all. Then he gave me some hay and some corn, and thinking he had done right, he went away.

Soon I began to shake and tremble, and turned deadly cold. My legs ached, my loins ached, and my chest ached, and I felt sore all over. Oh, how I wished for my warm thick cloth as I stood and trembled! I wished for John, but he had eight miles to walk, so I lay down in my straw and tried to go to sleep. After a long while I heard John at the door. I gave a low moan, for I was in great pain. He was at my side in a moment, stooping down by me. I could not tell him how I felt, but he seemed to know it all. He covered me up with two or three warm cloths, and then ran to the house for some hot water. He made me some warm gruel, which I drank, and then I think I went to sleep.

John seemed to be put out. I heard him say to himself over and over again, "Stupid boy! Stupid boy! No cloth put on, and I daresay the water was cold too. Boys are no good." But Joe was a good boy, after all.

I was now very ill. A strong inflammation had attacked my lungs, and I could not draw my breath without pain. John nursed me night and day. He would get up two or three times in the night to come to me. My master, too, often came to see me. "My poor Beauty," he said one day. "My good horse, you saved your mistress's life, Beauty! Yes, you saved her life." I was very glad to hear that, for it seems the doctor had said if we had been a little longer it would have been too late. John told my master he never saw a horse go so fast in his life.

CHAPTER XIX

Only Ignorance

I DO NOT KNOW HOW LONG I WAS ILL. MR. BOND, THE horse doctor, came every day. One day he bled me; John held a pail for the blood. I felt very faint after it, and thought I should die, and I believe they all thought so too.

Ginger and Merrylegs had been moved into the other stable so that I might be quiet, for the fever made me very quick of hearing. Any little noise seemed quite loud, and I could tell everyone's footstep going to and from the house. I knew all that was going on.

One night John had to give me a draft. Thomas Green came in to help him. After I had taken it and John had made me as comfortable as he could, he said he should stay half an hour to see how the medicine settled. Thomas said he would stay with him, so they went and sat down on a bench that had been brought into Merrylegs's stall, and put down the lantern at their feet that I might not be disturbed with the light.

For a while both men sat silent, and then Tom Green said in a low voice:

"I wish, John, you'd say a bit of a kind word to Joe. The boy is quite broken-hearted. He can't eat his meals, and he can't smile. He says he knows it was all his fault, though he is sure he did the best he knew, and he says, if Beauty dies, no one will ever speak to him again. It goes to my heart to hear him. I think you might give him just a word. He is not a bad boy."

After a short pause, John said slowly, "You must not be too hard upon me, Tom. I know he meant no harm, I never said he did. I know he is not a bad boy, but you see I am sore myself. That horse is the pride of my heart, to say nothing of his being such a favorite with the master and mistress; and to think that his life may be flung away in this manner is more than I can bear. But if you think I am hard on the boy, I will try to give him a good word tomorrow—that is, I mean if Beauty is better."

"Well, John, thank you! I knew you did not wish to be too hard, and I am glad you see it was only ignorance."

John's voice almost startled me as he answered, "*Only* ignorance! Only *ignorance!* How can you talk about *only* ignorance? *Don't you know that it is the worst thing in the world, next to wickedness?* And which does the most mischief heaven only knows. If people can say, 'Oh! I did not know, I did not mean any harm,' they think it is all right. I suppose Martha Mulwash did not mean to kill that baby when she dosed it with Dalby and soothing syrups; but she did kill it, and was tried for manslaughter."

"And served her right too," said Tom. "A woman should not undertake to nurse a tender little child without knowing what is good and what is bad for it."

"Bill Starkey," continued John, "did not mean to frighten his brother into fits when he dressed up like a ghost and ran after him in the moonlight, but he did; and that bright, handsome little fellow, that might have been the pride of any mother's heart, is just no better than an idiot, and never will be if he lives to be eighty years old. You were a good deal cut up yourself, Tom, two weeks ago, when those young ladies left your hothouse door open, with a frosty east wind blowing right in; you said it killed a good many of your plants."

"A good many!" said Tom. "There was not one of the tender cuttings that was not nipped off. I shall have to strike all over again, and the worst of it is that I don't know where to go to get fresh ones. I was nearly mad when I came in and saw what was done."

"And yet," said John, "I am sure the young ladies did not mean it; it was only ignorance!"

I heard no more of this conversation, for the medicine did well and sent me to sleep, and in the morning I felt much better. But I often thought of John's words when I came to know more of the world.

CHAPTER XX
Joe Green

JOE GREEN WENT ON VERY WELL. HE LEARNED QUICKLY, and was so attentive and careful that John began to trust him in many things; but, as I have said, he was small of his age, and it was seldom that he was allowed to exercise either Ginger or me. But it so happened one morning that John was out with Justice in the luggage cart, and the master wanted a note to be taken immediately to a gentleman's house, about three miles distant, and sent his orders for Joe to saddle me and take it, adding the caution that he was to ride steadily.

The note was delivered, and we were quietly returning till we came to the brickfield. Here we saw a cart heavily laden with bricks. The wheels had stuck fast in the stiff mud of some deep ruts, and the carter was shouting and flogging the two horses unmercifully. Joe pulled up. It was a sad sight. There were the two horses straining and struggling with all their might to drag the cart out, but they could not move it. The sweat streamed from their legs and flanks, their sides heaved, and every muscle was strained, while the man, fiercely pulling at the head of the forehorse, swore and lashed most brutally.

"Hold hard," said Joe. "Don't go on flogging the horses like that. The wheels are so stuck that they cannot move the cart." The man took no heed, but went on lashing.

"Stop! Pray stop," said Joe. "I'll help you to lighten the cart. They can't move it now."

"Mind your own business, you impudent young rascal, and I'll mind mine." The man was in a towering passion, and the worse for drink, and laid on the whip again. Joe turned my head, and the next moment we were going at a round gallop toward the house of the master brickmaker. I cannot say if John would have approved of our pace, but Joe and I were both of one mind, and so angry that we could not have gone slower.

The house stood close by the roadside. Joe knocked at the door and shouted, "Hulloa! Is Mr. Clay at home?" The door was opened, and Mr. Clay himself came out.

"Hulloa, young man! You seem in a hurry. Any orders from the Squire this morning?"

"No, Mr. Clay, but there's a fellow in your brickyard flogging two horses to death. I told him to stop and he wouldn't. I said I'd help him to lighten the cart, and he wouldn't, so I have come to tell you. Pray, sir, go." Joe's voice shook with excitement.

"Thank ye, my lad," said the man, running in for his hat, then pausing for a moment—"Will you give evidence of what you saw if I should bring the fellow up before a magistrate?"

"That I will," said Joe, "and glad too." The man was gone, and we were on our way home at a smart trot.

"Why, what's the matter with you, Joe? You look angry all over," said John as the boy flung himself from the saddle.

"I am angry all over, I can tell you," said the boy, and then in hurried, excited words he told all that had happened. Joe was usually such a quiet, gentle little fellow that it was wonderful to see him so roused.

"Right, Joe! You did right, my boy, whether the fellow gets a summons or not. Many folks would have ridden by and said 'twas not their business to interfere. *Now I say that with cruelty and oppression it is everybody's business to interfere when they see it. You did right, my boy.*"

Joe was quite calm by this time, and proud that John approved of him, and he cleaned out my feet, and rubbed me down with a firmer hand than usual.

They were just going home to dinner when the footman came down to the stable to say that Joe was wanted directly in master's private room; there was a man brought up for ill-using horses, and Joe's evidence was wanted. The boy flushed up to his forehead, and his eyes sparkled. "They shall have it," said he.

"Put yourself a bit straight," said John. Joe gave a pull at his necktie and a twitch at his jacket, and was off in a moment. Our master being one of the county magistrates, cases were often brought to him to settle, or say what should be done. In the stable we heard no more for some time, as it was the men's dinner hour. But when Joe came next into the stable I saw he was in high spirits. He gave me a good-natured slap and said, "We won't see such things done, will we, old fellow?" We heard afterward that he had given his evidence so clearly, and the horses were in such an exhausted state, bearing marks of such brutal usage, that the carter was committed to take his trial, and might possibly be sentenced to two or three months in prison.

It was wonderful what a change had come over Joe. John laughed and said he had grown an inch taller in that week, and I believe he had. He was just as kind and gentle as before, but there was more purpose and determination in all that he did—as if he had jumped all at once from a boy into a man.

CHAPTER XXI

The Parting

I HAD NOW LIVED IN THIS HAPPY PLACE THREE YEARS, but sad changes were about to come over us. We heard from time to time that our mistress was ill. The doctor was often at the house, and the master looked grave and anxious. Then we heard that she must leave home at once and go to a warm country for two or three years. The news fell upon the household like the tolling of a death-bell. Everybody was sorry, but the master began directly to make arrangements for breaking up his establishment and leaving England. We used to hear it talked about in our stable—indeed, nothing else was talked about.

John went about his work silent and sad, and Joe scarcely whistled. There was a great deal of coming and going. Ginger and I had full work.

The first of the party who went were Miss Jessie and Flora with their governess. They came to bid us goodbye. They hugged poor

Merrylegs like an old friend, and so indeed he was. Then we heard what had been arranged for us. Master had sold Ginger and me to his old friend, the Earl of W——, for he thought we should have a good place there. Merrylegs he had given to the Vicar, who was wanting a pony for Mrs. Bloomfield, but it was *on the condition that he should never be sold, and when he was past work that he should be shot and buried.*

Joe was engaged to take care of him and to help in the house, so I thought Merrylegs was well off. John had the offer of several good places, but he said he should wait a little and look around.

The evening before they left, the master came into the stable to give some directions and to give his horses the last pat. He seemed very low-spirited; I knew that by his voice. I believe we horses can tell more by the voice than many men can.

"Have you decided what to do, John?" he said. "I find you have not accepted any of those offers."

"No, sir. I have made up my mind that if I could get a situation with some first-rate colt-breaker and horse-trainer, it would be the right thing for me. Many young animals are frightened and spoiled by wrong treatment, which need not be if the right man took them in hand. I always get on well with horses, and if I could help some of them to a fair start I should feel as if I was doing some good. What do you think of it, sir?"

"I don't know a man anywhere," said master, "that I should think so suitable for it as yourself. You understand horses, and somehow they understand you, and in time you might set up for yourself. I think you could not do better. If in any way I can help you, write to me. I shall speak to my agent in London and leave your character with him."

Master gave John the name and address, and then he thanked him for his long and faithful service. But that was too much for John. "Pray don't, sir, I can't bear it; you and my dear mistress have done so much for me that I could never repay it. But we shall never forget you, sir, and please God we may someday see mistress back again like herself. We must keep up hope, sir." Master gave John his hand, but he did not speak, and they both left the stable.

The last sad day had come. The footman and the heavy luggage had gone off the day before, and there was only master and mistress and her maid. Ginger and I brought the carriage up to the Hall door for the last time.

The servants brought out cushions and rugs and many other things, and when all were arranged, master came down the steps carrying the mistress in his arms (I was on the side next to the house and could see all that went on). He placed her carefully in the carriage while the house servants stood around crying.

"Good-bye again," he said, "we shall not forget any of you." And he got in. "Drive on, John."

Joe jumped up, and we trotted slowly through the park and through the village, where the people were standing at their doors to have a last look and to say "God bless them."

When we reached the railway station I think mistress walked from the carriage to the waiting room. I heard her say in her own sweet voice, "Good-bye, John. God bless you." I felt the rein twitch, but John made no answer. Perhaps he could not speak. As soon as Joe had taken the things out of the carriage, John called him to stand by the horses while he went on the platform. Poor Joe! He stood close up to our heads to hide his tears. Very soon the train came puffing up into the station; then two or three minutes and the doors were slammed to, the guard whistled, and the train glided away, leaving behind it only clouds of white smoke and some very heavy hearts.

When it was quite out of sight, John came back.

"We shall never see her again," he said, "never." He took the reins, mounted the box, and with Joe drove slowly home. But it was not our home now.

Part Two

CHAPTER XXII

Earlshall

THE NEXT MORNING AFTER BREAKFAST, JOE PUT Merrylegs into the mistress's low chaise to take him to the vicarage. He came first and said good-bye to us, and Merrylegs neighed to us from the yard. Then John put the saddle on Ginger and the leading rein on me, and rode us across the country about fifteen miles to Earlshall Park, where the Earl of W—— lived. There was a very fine house and a great deal of stabling. We went into the yard through a stone gateway, and John asked for Mr. York. It was some time before he came. He was a fine-looking middle-aged man, and his voice said at once that he expected to be obeyed. He was very friendly and polite to John, and after giving us a slight look he called a groom to take us to our boxes, and invited John to take some refreshment.

We were taken to a light, airy stable and placed in boxes adjoining each other, where we were rubbed down and fed. In about half an hour John and Mr. York, who was to be our new coachman, came in to see us.

"Now, Mr. Manly," he said, after carefully looking at us both, "I can see no fault in these horses, but we all know that horses have their peculiarities as well as men, and that sometimes they need different treatment. I should like to know if there is anything particular in either of these that you would like to mention."

"Well," said John, "I don't believe there is a better pair of horses in the country, and right grieved I am to part with them, but they are not alike. The black one has the most perfect temper I ever knew. I suppose he has never known a hard word or a blow since he was foaled, and all his pleasure seems to be to do what you wish. But the chestnut, I fancy, must have had bad treatment; we heard as much from the dealer. She came to us snappish and suspicious, but when she found what sort of place ours was, it all went off by degrees; for three years I have never seen the smallest sign of temper, and if she is well treated, there is not a better, more willing animal than she is, but she is naturally of a more irritable constitution than the black horse. Flies tease her more, anything wrong in the harness frets her more, and if she were ill-used or unfairly treated she would not be unlikely to give tit for tat. You know that many high-mettled horses will do so."

"Of course," said York, "I quite understand, but you know it is not easy in stables like these to have all the grooms just what they should be. I do my best, and there I must leave it. I'll remember what you have said about the mare."

They were going out of the stable when John stopped and said, "I had better mention that we have never used the checkrein with either of them. The black horse never had one on, and the dealer said it was the gag-bit that spoiled the other's temper."

"Well," said York, "if they come here they must wear the check-rein. *I prefer a loose rein myself, and his lordship is always very reasonable about horses; but my lady—that's another thing;* she will have style, and if her carriage horses are not reined up tight she wouldn't look at them. I always stand out against the gag-bit, and shall do so, but *it must be tight up when my lady rides!*"

"I am sorry for it, very sorry," said John, "but I must go now, or I shall lose the train."

He came round to each of us to pat and speak to us for the last time. His voice sounded very sad.

I held my face close to him; that was all I could do to say good-bye. And then he was gone, and I have never seen him since.

The next day Lord W—— came to look at us. He seemed pleased with our appearance.

"I have great confidence in these horses," he said, "from the character my friend Mr. Gordon has given me of them. Of course they are not a match in color, but my idea is that they will do very well for the carriage while we are in the country. Before we go to London I must try to match Baron. The black horse, I believe, is perfect for riding."

York then told him what John had said about us.

"Well," said he, "you must keep an eye to the mare, and put the check-rein easy. I daresay they will do very well with a little humoring at first. I'll mention it to your lady."

In the afternoon we were harnessed and put in the carriage, and as the stable clock struck three we were led round to the front of the house. It was all very grand, and three or four times as large as the old house at Birtwick, but not half so pleasant, if a horse may have an opinion. Two footmen were standing ready, dressed in drab livery, with scarlet breeches and white stockings.

Presently we heard the rustling sound of silk as my lady came down the flight of stone steps. She stepped around to look at us. She was a tall, proud-looking woman, and did not seem pleased about something, but she said nothing and got into the carriage. This was the first time of wearing a check-rein, and I must say, though it certainly was a nuisance not to be able to get my head down now and then, it did not pull my head higher than I was accustomed to carry it. I felt anxious about Ginger, but she seemed to be quiet and content.

The next day at three o'clock we were again at the door, and the footmen as before. We heard the silk dress rustle, and the lady came down the steps, and in an imperious voice she said, *"York, you must put those horses' heads higher. They are not fit to be seen."*

York got down and said very respectfully, "I beg your pardon, my lady, but these horses have not been reined up for three years, and my lord said it would be safer to bring them to it by degrees; but if your ladyship pleases, I can take them up a little more."

"Do so," she said.

York came round to our heads and shortened the rein himself, one hole, I think. Every little makes a difference, be it for better or worse, and that day we had a steep hill to go up. Then I began to understand what I had heard of.

Of course I wanted to put my head forward and take the carriage up with a will, as we had been used to do. But no, I had to pull my head up now, and *that took all the spirit out of me, and the strain came on my back and legs.* When we came in, Ginger said,

"Now you see what it is like, but this is not bad, and if it does not get much worse than this I shall say nothing about it, for we are very well treated here. But if they strain me up tight, why, let 'em look out! I can't bear it, and I won't."

Day by day, hole by hole, our bearing reins were shortened, and instead of looking forward with pleasure to having my harness put on, as I used to do, I began to dread it. Ginger, too, seemed restless, though she said very little. At last I thought the worst was over; for several days there was no more shortening, and I determined to make the best of it and do my duty, though it was now a constant harass instead of a pleasure; but the worst was not yet come.

CHAPTER XXIII

A Strike for Liberty

ONE DAY MY LADY CAME DOWN LATER THAN USUAL, and the silk rustled more than ever.

"Drive to the Duchess of B——'s," she said, and then, after a pause, "Are you never going to get those horses' heads up, York? Raise them at once, and let us have no more of this humoring and nonsense."

York came to me first, while the groom stood at Ginger's head. *He drew my head back and fixed the rein so tight that it was almost intolerable,* then he went to Ginger, who was impatiently jerking her head up and down against the bit, as was her way now. She had a good idea of what was coming, and the moment York took the rein off the terret in order to shorten it she took her opportunity and reared up so suddenly that York had his nose roughly hit and his hat knocked off; the groom was nearly thrown off his legs. At once they both flew to her head, but she was a match for them and went on plunging, rearing, and kicking in a most desperate manner. At last she kicked right over the carriage pole and fell down, after giving me a severe blow on my near quarter. There is no knowing what farther mischief she might have done had not York promptly sat himself down flat on her head to prevent her struggling, at the same time calling out, "Unbuckle the black horse! Run for the winch and unscrew the carriage pole. Cut the trace here, somebody, if you can't unhitch it." One of the footmen ran for the winch, and another brought a knife from the house.

The groom soon set me free from Ginger and the carriage, and led me to my box. He just turned me in as I was, and ran back to York. I was very much excited by what had happened, and if I had ever been used to kick or rear, I am sure I should have done it then. But I never had, and there I stood angry, sore in my leg, my head still strained up to the terret on the saddle, and no power to get it down. I was very miserable, and felt much inclined to kick the first person who came near me.

Before long, however, Ginger was led in by two grooms, a good deal knocked about and bruised. York came with her and gave his orders, and then came to look at me. In a moment he let down my head.

"Confound these check-reins!" he said to himself. "I thought we should have some mischief soon. Master will be sorely vexed. But here, if a woman's husband can't rule her, of course a servant can't; so I wash my hands of it, and if she can't get to the Duchess's garden party I can't help it."

York did not say this before the men; he always spoke respectfully when they were by. Now he felt me all over, and soon found the place above my hock where I had been kicked. It was swelled and painful; he ordered it to be sponged with hot water, and then some lotion was put on.

Lord W—— was much put out when he learned what had happened. He blamed York for giving way to his mistress, to which he replied that in future he would much prefer to receive his orders only from his lordship. But I think nothing came of it, for things went on the same as before. I thought York might have stood up better for his horses, but perhaps I am no judge.

Ginger was never put into the carriage again, but when she was well of her bruises one of Lord W——'s younger sons said he should like to have her. He was sure she would make a good hunter. As for me, I was obliged still to go in the carriage, and had a fresh partner called Max. He had always been used to the tight rein. I asked him how it was he bore it.

"Well," he said, "I bear it because I must, but it is shortening my life, and it will shorten yours too, if you have to stick to it."

"Do you think," I said, "that our masters know how bad it is for us?"

"I can't say," he replied, "but the dealers and the horse doctors know it very well. I was at a dealer's once, who was training me and another horse to go as a pair. He was getting our heads up, as he said, a little higher every day. A gentleman who was there asked him why he did so. 'Because,' said he, 'people won't buy them unless we do. The London people always want their horses to carry their heads high and to step high. Of course it is very bad for the horses, *but then it is good for trade.* The horses soon wear up, or get diseased, and they come for another pair.' That," said Max, "is what he said in my hearing, and you can judge for yourself."

What I suffered with that rein for four long months in my lady's carriage it would be hard to describe, but I am quite sure that, had it lasted much longer, either my health or my temper would have given way. Before that, I never knew what it was to foam at the mouth, but now the action of the sharp bit on my tongue and jaw, and the constrained position of my head and throat, always caused me to froth at the mouth more or less. Some people think it is very fine to see this, and say, "What fine, spirited creatures!" *But it is just as unnatural for horses as for men to foam at the mouth;* it is a sure sign of some discomfort and should be attended to. Besides this, there was a pressure on my windpipe, which often made my breathing very uncomfortable. When I returned from my work, my neck and chest were strained and painful, my mouth and tongue tender, and I felt worn and depressed.

In my old home I always knew that John and my master were my friends; but here, although in many ways I was well treated, I had no friend. York might have known, and very likely did know, how that rein harassed me, but I suppose he took it as a matter of course that could not be helped. At any rate, nothing was done to relieve me.

CHAPTER XXIV

The Lady Anne, or A Runaway Horse

EARLY IN THE SPRING, LORD W—— AND PART OF his family went up to London and took York with them. I and Ginger and some other horses were left at home for use, and the head groom was left in charge.

The Lady Harriet, who remained at the Hall, was a great invalid, and never went out in the carriage, and the Lady Anne preferred riding on horseback with her brother or cousins. She was a perfect horsewoman, and as gay and gentle as she was beautiful. She chose me for her horse and named me "Black Auster." I enjoyed these rides very much in the clear, cold air, sometimes with Ginger, sometimes with Lizzie. This Lizzie was a bright bay mare, almost thoroughbred, and a great favorite with the gentlemen, on account of her fine action and lively spirit; but Ginger, who knew more of her than I did, told me she was rather nervous.

There was a gentleman of the name of Blantyre staying at the

Hall. He always rode Lizzie, and praised her so much that one day Lady Anne ordered the sidesaddle to be put on her and the other saddle on me. When we came to the door, the gentleman seemed very uneasy.

"How is this?" he said. "Are you tired of your good Black Auster?"

"Oh, no, not at all!" she replied. "But I am amiable enough to let you ride him for once, and I will try your charming Lizzie. You must confess that in size and appearance she is far more like a lady's horse than my own favorite."

"Do let me advise you not to mount her," he said. "She is a charming creature, but she is too nervous for a lady. I assure you, she is not perfectly safe. Let me beg you to have the saddles changed."

"My dear cousin," said Lady Anne, laughing, "pray do not trouble your good careful head about me. I have been a horsewoman ever since I was a baby, and I have followed the hounds a great many times, though I know you do not approve of ladies hunting. But still that is the fact, and I intend to try this Lizzie that you gentlemen are all so fond of, so please help me to mount, like a good friend as you are."

There was no more to be said. He placed her carefully on the saddle, looked to the bit and curb, gave the reins gently into her hand, and then mounted me. Just as we were moving off, a footman came out with a slip of paper and message from the Lady Harriet. "Would they ask this question for her at Dr. Ashley's, and bring the answer?"

The village was about a mile off, and the doctor's house was the last in it. We went along gaily enough till we came to his gate. There was a short drive up to the house between tall evergreens.

Blantyre alighted at the gate, and was going to open it for Lady Anne, but she said, "I will wait for you here, and you can hang Auster's rein on the gate."

He looked at her doubtfully. "I will not be five minutes," he said.

"Oh, do not hurry yourself. Lizzie and I shall not run away from you."

He hung my rein on one of the iron spikes, and was soon hidden among the trees. Lizzie was standing quietly by the side of the road a few paces off with her back to me. My young mistress was sitting easily with a loose rein, humming a little song. I listened to my rider's footsteps until they reached the house, and heard him knock at the door. There was a meadow on the opposite side of the road, the gate of which stood open. Just then some cart horses and several young colts came trotting out in a very disorderly manner, while a boy behind was cracking a great whip. The colts were wild and frolicsome, and one of them bolted across the road and blundered up against Lizzie's hind legs. Whether it was the stupid colt, or the loud cracking of the whip, or both together, I cannot say, but she gave a violent kick and dashed off into a headlong gallop. It was so sudden that Lady Anne was nearly unseated, but she soon recovered herself.

I gave a loud, shrill neigh for help. Again and again I neighed, pawing the ground impatiently and tossing my head to get the rein loose. I had not long to wait. Blantyre came running to the gate. He looked anxiously about, and just caught sight of the flying figure, now far away on the road. In an instant he sprang to the saddle. I needed no whip, nor spur, for I was as eager as my rider. He saw it, and giving me a free rein, and leaning a little forward, we dashed after them.

For about a mile and a half the road ran straight, and then bent to the right, after which it divided into two roads. Long before we came to the bend, she was out of sight. Which way had she turned? A woman was standing at her garden gate, shading her eyes with her hand and looking eagerly up the road. Scarcely drawing the rein, Blantyre shouted, "Which way?" "To the right," cried the woman, pointing with her hand, and away we went up the right-hand road, then for a moment we caught sight of her; another bend and she was hidden again. Several times we caught glimpses, and then lost them. We scarcely seemed to gain ground upon them at all.

An old road mender was standing near a heap of stones; his shovel dropped and his hands raised. As we came near he made a sign to speak. Blantyre drew rein a little. "To the common, to the common, sir; she has turned off there." I knew this common very well; it was for the most part very uneven ground, covered with heather and dark green furze bushes, with here and there a scrubby old thorn tree. There were also open spaces of fine short grass, with ant-hills and mole-turns everywhere—the worst place I ever knew for a headlong gallop.

We had hardly turned on the common, when we caught sight again of the green habit flying on before us. My lady's hat was gone, and her long brown hair was streaming behind her. Her head and body were thrown back, as if she were pulling with all her remaining strength, and as if that strength were nearly exhausted. It was clear that the roughness of the ground had very much lessened Lizzie's speed, and there seemed a chance that we might overtake her.

While we were on the high-road, Blantyre had given me my head; but now, with a light hand and a practiced eye, he guided me over the ground in such a masterly manner that my pace was scarcely slackened, and we were decidedly gaining on them.

About halfway across the heath there had been a wide dike recently cut, and the earth from the cutting was cast up roughly on the other side. Surely this would stop them! But no. With scarcely a pause Lizzie took the leap, stumbled among the rough clods, and fell. Blantyre groaned, "Now, Auster, do your best!" He gave me a steady rein. I gathered myself well together and with one determined leap cleared both dike and bank.

Motionless among the heather, with her face to the earth, lay my poor young mistress. Blantyre kneeled down and called her name; there was no sound. Gently he turned her face upward; it was ghastly white, and the eyes were closed. "Annie, dear Annie, do speak!" but there was no answer. He unbuttoned her habit, loosened her collar, felt her hands and wrists, then started up and looked wildly round him for help.

At no great distance there were two men cutting turf, who, seeing Lizzie running wild without a rider, had left their work to catch her.

Blantyre's halloo soon brought them to the spot. The foremost man seemed much troubled at the sight and asked what he could do.

"Can you ride?"

"Well, sir, I bean't much of a horseman, but I'd risk my neck for Lady Anne; she was uncommon good to my wife in the winter."

"Then mount this horse, my friend—your neck will be quite safe—and ride to the doctor's and ask him to come instantly—then on to the Hall—tell them all that you know, and bid them send me the carriage with Lady Anne's maid and help. I shall stay here."

"All right, sir, I'll do my best, and I pray God the dear young lady may open her eyes soon." Then, seeing the other man, he called out, "Here, Joe, run for some water, and tell my missus to come as quick as she can to the Lady Anne."

He then somehow scrambled into the saddle, and with a "Gee-up" and a clap on my sides with both his legs, he started on his journey, making a little circuit to avoid the dike. He had no whip, which seemed to trouble him, but my pace soon cured that difficulty, and he found the best thing he could do was to stick to the saddle and hold me in, which he did manfully. I shook him as little as I could help, but once or twice on the rough ground he called out, "Steady! Whoa! Steady!" On the high-road we were all right, and at the doctor's and the Hall he did his errand like a good man and true. They asked him in to take a drop of something. "No, no!" he said. "I'll be back to 'em again by a short cut through the fields, and be there afore the carriage."

There was a great deal of hurry and excitement after the news became known. I was just turned into my box; the saddle and the bridle were taken off, and a cloth thrown over me.

Ginger was saddled and sent off in great haste for Lord George, and I soon heard the carriage roll out of the yard.

It seemed a long time before Ginger came back, and before we were left alone, and then she told me all that she had seen.

"I can't tell much," she said. "We went at a gallop nearly all the way, and got there just as the doctor rode up. There was a woman sitting on the ground with the lady's head in her lap. The doctor poured something into her mouth, but all that I heard was, 'She is not dead.' Then I was led off by a man to a little distance. After a while she was taken to the carriage, and we came home together. I heard my master say to a gentleman who stopped him to inquire, that he hoped no bones were broken, but that she had not spoken yet."

When Lord George took Ginger for hunting, York shook his head. He said it ought to be a steady hand to train a horse for the first season, and not a random rider like Lord George.

Ginger used to like it very much, but sometimes when she came back I could see that she had been very much strained, and now and then she gave a short cough. She had too much spirit to complain, but I could not help feeling anxious about her.

Two days after the accident, Blantyre paid me a visit. He patted me and praised me very much; he told Lord George that he was sure the horse knew of Annie's danger as well as he did. "I could not have held him in if I would," said he. "She ought never to ride any other horse." I found by their conversation that my young mistress was now out of danger, and would soon be able to ride again. This was good news to me, and I looked forward to a happy life.

CHAPTER XXV

Reuben Smith

I MUST NOW SAY A LITTLE ABOUT REUBEN SMITH, who was left in charge of the stables when York went to London. No one more thoroughly understood his business than he did, and when he was all right, there could not be a more faithful or valuable man. He was gentle and very clever in his management of horses, and could doctor them almost as well as a farrier, for he had lived two years with a veterinary surgeon. He was a first-rate driver; he could take a four-in-hand or a tandem as easily as a pair. He was a handsome man, a good scholar, and had very pleasant manners. I believe everybody liked him; certainly the horses did.

The only wonder was that he should be in an under situation, and not in the place of a head coachman like York. But he had one great fault, and that was the love of drink. He was not like some men, always at it; he used to keep steady for weeks or months together, and then he would break out and have a "bout" of it, as

York called it, and be a disgrace to himself, a terror to his wife, and a nuisance to all that had to do with him. He was, however, so useful that two or three times York had hushed the matter up, and kept it from the Earl's knowledge. But one night, when Reuben had to drive a party home from a ball, he was so drunk that he could not hold the reins, and a gentleman of the party had to mount the box and drive the ladies home.

Of course this could not be hidden, and Reuben was at once dismissed. His poor wife and little children had to turn out of the pretty cottage by the park gate and go where they could. Old Max told me all this, for it happened a good while ago, but shortly before Ginger and I came, Smith had been taken back again. York had interceded for him with the Earl, who is very kind-hearted, and the man had promised faithfully that he would never taste another drop as long as he lived there. He had kept his promise so well that York thought he might be safely trusted to fill his place while he was away, and he was so clever and honest that no one else seemed so well fitted for it.

It was now early in April, and the family was expected home some time in May. The light brougham was to be freshly done up, and as Colonel Blantyre was obliged to return to his regiment, it was arranged that Smith should drive him to the town in it, and ride back. For this purpose, he took the saddle with him, and I was chosen for the journey. At the station the Colonel put some money into Smith's hand and bid him good-bye, saying, "Take care of your young mistress, Reuben, and don't let Black Auster be hacked about by any random young prig that wants to ride him—keep him for the lady."

We left the carriage at the maker's, and Smith rode me to the White Lion and ordered the ostler to feed me well and have me ready for him at four o'clock. A nail in one of my front shoes had started as I came along, but the ostler did not notice it till just about four o'clock. Smith did not come into the yard till five, and then he said he should not leave till six, as he had met with some old friends. The man then told him of the nail, and asked if he should have the shoe looked to.

"No," said Smith, "that will be all right till we get home."

He spoke in a very loud, off-hand way, and I thought it very unlike him not to see about the shoe, as he was generally wonderfully particular about loose nails in our shoes. He did not come at six, or seven, or eight, and it was nearly nine o'clock before he called for me, and then it was with a loud, rough voice. He seemed in a very bad temper, and abused the ostler, though I could not tell what for.

The landlord stood at the door and said, "Have a care, Mr. Smith!" But he answered angrily with an oath, and almost before he was out of the town he began to gallop, frequently giving me a sharp cut with his whip, though I was going at full speed. The moon had not yet risen, and it was very dark. The roads were stony, having been recently mended. Going over them at this pace, my shoe became looser, and when we were near the turnpike gate it came off.

If Smith had been in his right senses, he would have been sensible of something wrong in my pace, but he was too madly drunk to notice anything.

Beyond the turnpike was a long piece of road, upon which fresh stones had just been laid—large, sharp stones, over which no horse could be driven quickly without risk of danger. Over this road, with one shoe gone, I was forced to gallop at my utmost speed, my rider meanwhile cutting into me with his whip, and with wild curses urging me to go still faster. Of course my shoeless foot suffered dreadfully. The hoof was broken and split down to the very quick, and the inside was terribly cut by the sharpness of the stones.

This could not go on; no horse could keep his footing under such circumstances, the pain was too great. I stumbled, and fell with violence on both my knees. Smith was flung off by my fall, and owing to the speed I was going at, he must have fallen with great force. I soon recovered my feet and limped to the side of the road, where it was free from stones. The moon had just risen above the hedge, and by its light I could see Smith lying a few yards beyond me. He did not rise; he made one slight effort to do so, and then there was a heavy groan. I could have groaned, too, for I was suffering intense pain both from my foot and knees, but horses are used to bearing their pain in silence. I uttered no sound, but I stood there and listened. One more heavy groan from Smith, but though he now lay in the full moonlight I could see no motion. I could do nothing for him or myself, but oh, how I listened for the sound of a horse, or wheels, or footsteps!

The road was not much frequented, and at this time of the night we might stay for hours before help came to us. I stood watching and listening. It was a calm, sweet April night. There were no sounds but a few low notes of a nightingale, and nothing moved but the white clouds near the moon and a brown owl that flitted over the hedge. It made me think of the summer nights long ago when I used to lie beside my mother in the green pleasant meadow at Farmer Grey's.

CHAPTER XXVI

How It Ended

IT MUST HAVE BEEN NEARLY MIDNIGHT WHEN I heard at a great distance the sound of a horse's feet. Sometimes the sound died away, then it grew clearer again and nearer. The road to Earlshall led through plantations that belonged to the Earl; the sound came from that direction, and I hoped it might be someone coming in search of us. As the sound came nearer and nearer, I was almost sure I could distinguish Ginger's step; a little nearer still, and I could tell she was in the dog-cart. I neighed loudly, and was overjoyed to hear an answering neigh from Ginger and men's voices. They came slowly over the stones, and stopped at the dark figure that lay upon the ground.

One of the men jumped out and stooped down over it. "It is Reuben!" he said. "And he does not stir."

The other man followed and bent over him. "He's dead," he said. "Feel how cold his hands are."

They raised him up, but there was no life, and his hair was soaked with blood. They laid him down again, and came and looked at me. They soon saw my cut knees.

"Why, the horse has been down and thrown him! Who would have thought the black horse would have done that? Nobody thought he could fall. Reuben must have been lying here for hours! Odd, too, that the horse has not moved from the place."

Robert then attempted to lead me forward. I made a step, but almost fell again.

"Halloo! He's bad in his foot as well as his knees. Look here—his hoof is cut all to pieces; he might well come down, poor fellow! I tell you what, Ned, I'm afraid it hasn't been all right with Reuben. Just think of him riding a horse over these stones without a shoe! Why, if he had been in his right senses he would just as soon have tried to ride him over the moon. I'm afraid it has been the old thing over again. Poor Susan! She looked awfully pale when she came to my house to ask if he had not come home. She made believe she was not a bit anxious, and talked of a lot of things that might have kept him. But for all that, she begged me to go and meet him. But what must we do? There's the horse to get home as well as the body, and that will be no easy matter."

Then followed a conversation between them, till it was agreed that Robert, as the groom, should lead me, and that Ned must take the body. It was a hard job to get it into the dog-cart, for there was no one to hold Ginger. But she knew as well as I did what was going on, and stood as still as a stone. I noticed that, because, if she had a fault, it was that she was impatient in standing.

Ned started off very slowly with his sad load, and Robert came and looked at my foot again; then he took his handkerchief and bound it closely round, and so he led me home. I shall never forget that night walk; it was more than three miles. Robert led me on very slowly, and I limped and hobbled on as well as I could with great pain. I am sure he was sorry for me, for he often patted and encouraged me, talking to me in a pleasant voice.

At last I reached my own box, and had some corn. After Robert had wrapped up my knees in wet clothes, he tied up my foot in a bran poultice, to draw out the heat and cleanse it before the horse doctor saw it in the morning, and I managed to get myself down on the straw, and slept in spite of the pain.

The next day, after the farrier had examined my wounds, he said he hoped the joint was not injured; and if so, I should not be spoiled for work, but I should never lose the blemish. I believe they did the best to make a good cure, but it was a long and painful one. Proud flesh, as they called it, came up in my knees, and was burned out with caustic, and when at last it was healed, they put a blistering fluid over the front of both knees to bring all the hair off. They had some reason for this, and I suppose it was all right.

As Smith's death had been so sudden, and no one was there to see it, there was an inquest held. The landlord and ostler at the White Lion, with several other people, gave evidence that he was intoxicated when he started from the inn. The keeper of the toll-gate said he rode at a hard gallop through the gate; and my shoe was picked up among the stones, so that the case was quite plain to them, and I was cleared of all blame.

Everybody pitied Susan. She was nearly out of her mind. She kept saying over and over again, "Oh, he was so good—so good! It was all that cursed drink. Why will they sell that cursed drink?

Oh, Reuben, Reuben!" So she went on till after he was buried; and then, as she had no home or relations, she, with her six little children, was obliged once more to leave the pleasant home by the tall oak trees and go into that great, gloomy Union House.

CHAPTER XXVII

Ruined, and Going Downhill

AS SOON AS MY KNEES WERE SUFFICIENTLY HEALED, I was turned out into a small meadow for a month or two. No other creature was there, and though I enjoyed the liberty and the sweet grass, yet I had been so long used to society that I felt very lonely. Ginger and I had become fast friends, and now I missed her company extremely. I often neighed when I heard horses' feet passing in the road, but I seldom got an answer, till one morning the gate was opened, and who should come in but dear old Ginger. The man slipped off her halter and left her there. With a joyful whinny I trotted up to her; we were both glad to meet, but I soon found that it was not for our pleasure that she was brought to be with me. Her story would be too long to tell, but the end of it was that she had been ruined by hard riding, and was now turned off to see what rest would do.

Lord George was young and would take no warning. He was a hard rider, and would hunt whenever he could get the chance, quite careless of his horse. Soon after I left the stable there was a steeplechase, and he determined to ride. Though the groom told him she was a little strained, and was not fit for the race, he did not believe it, and on the day of the race urged Ginger to keep up with the foremost riders. With her high spirit, she strained herself to the utmost. She came in with the first three horses, but her wind was touched, beside which he was too heavy for her, and her back was strained. “And so,” she said, “here we are, ruined in the prime of our youth and strength, you by a drunkard and I by a fool. It is very hard.”

We both felt in ourselves that we were not what we had been. However, that did not spoil the pleasure we had in each other’s company. We did not gallop about as we once did, but we used to feed and lie down together, and stand for hours under one of the shady lime-trees with our heads close to each other. And so we passed our time till the family returned from town.

One day we saw the Earl come into the meadow, and York was with him. Seeing who it was, we stood still under our lime-tree, and let them come up to us. They examined us carefully. The Earl seemed much annoyed.

“There is three hundred pounds flung away for no earthly use,” said he, “but what I care most for is that these horses of my old friend, who thought they would find a good home with me, are ruined. The mare shall have a twelve months’ run, and we shall see what that will do for her, but the black one must be sold. ’Tis a great pity, but I could not have knees like these in my stables.”

“No, my lord, of course not,” said York, “but he might get a place where appearance is not of much consequence, and still be well treated. I know a man in Bath, the master of some livery stables, who often wants a good horse at a low figure. I know he looks well after his horses. The inquest cleared the horse's character, and your lordship's recommendation or mine would be sufficient warrant for him."

"You had better write to him, York. I should be more particular about the place than the money he would fetch."

After this they left us.

"They'll soon take you away," said Ginger, "and I shall lose the only friend I have, and most likely we shall never see each other again. 'Tis a hard world!"

About a week after this, Robert came into the field with a halter, which he slipped over my head, and led me away.

There was no leave-taking of Ginger; we neighed to each other as I was led off, and she trotted anxiously along the hedge, calling to me as long as she could hear the sound of my feet.

Through the recommendation of York I was bought by the master of the livery stables. I had to go by train, which was new to me, and required a good deal of courage the first time; but as I found the puffing, rushing, whistling, and, more than all, the trembling of the horse box in which I stood did me no real harm, I soon took it quietly.

When I reached the end of my journey I found myself in a tolerably comfortable stable, and well attended to. These stables were not so airy and pleasant as those I had been used to. The stalls were laid on a slope instead of being level, and as my head was kept tied to the manger, *I was obliged always to stand on the slope, which was very fatiguing.* Men do not seem to know yet that horses can do more work if they can stand comfortably and can turn about; however, I was well fed and well cleaned, and, on the whole, I think my master took as much care of us as he could. He kept a good many horses and carriages of different kinds for hire. Sometimes his own men drove them; at others, the horse and chaise were let to gentlemen or ladies who themselves drove.

CHAPTER XXVIII

A Job Horse and His Drivers

HITHERTO I HAD ALWAYS BEEN DRIVEN BY PEOPLE who at least knew how to drive; but in this place I was to get my experience of all the different kinds of bad and ignorant driving to which we horses are subjected. For I was a "job horse," and was let out to all sorts of people who wished to hire me; and as I was good-tempered and gentle, I think I was oftener let out to the ignorant drivers than some of the other horses, because I could be depended upon. It would take a long time to tell of all the different styles in which I was driven, but I will mention a few of them.

First there were the *tight-rein drivers*—men who seemed to think that all depended on holding the reins as hard as they could, never relaxing the pull on the horse's mouth, or giving him the least liberty of movement. They are always talking about "keeping the horse well in hand" and "holding a horse up," just as if a horse was not made *to hold himself up*.

Some poor, broken-down horses, whose mouths have been made hard and insensible by just such drivers as these, may perhaps find some support in it; but for a horse who can depend upon his own legs, and who has a tender mouth, and is easily guided, it is not only tormenting, but it is stupid.

Then there are the *loose-rein drivers,* who let the reins lie easily on our backs, and their own hands rest lazily on their knees. Of course, such gentlemen have no control over a horse, if anything happens suddenly. If a horse shies, or starts, or stumbles, they are nowhere, and cannot help the horse or themselves till the mischief is done. Of course, for myself, I had no objection to it, as I was not in the habit either of starting or stumbling, and had only been used to depend on my driver for guidance and encouragement; still, one likes to feel the rein a little in going downhill and likes to know that one's driver has not gone to sleep.

Besides, a slovenly way of driving gets a horse into bad and often lazy habits, and when he changes hands he has to be whipped out of them with more or less pain and trouble. Squire Gordon always kept us to our best paces and our best manners. He said that spoiling a horse and letting him get into bad habits was just as cruel as spoiling a child, and both had to suffer for it afterward.

Besides, these drivers are often careless altogether, and will attend to anything else more than their horses. I went out in the phaeton one day with one of them; he had a lady and two children behind. He flopped the reins about as we started, and of course gave me several unmeaning cuts with the whip, though I was fairly off. There had been a good deal of road-mending going on, and even where the stones were not freshly laid down there were a great many loose ones about. My driver was laughing and joking with the lady and the children, and talking about the country to the right and the left; but he never thought it worthwhile to keep an eye on his horse, or *to drive on the smoothest parts of the road;* and so it easily happened that I got a stone in one of my forefeet.

Now, if Mr. Gordon, or John, or in fact any good driver, had been there, he would have seen that something was wrong before I had gone three paces. Or even if it had been dark, a practiced hand would have felt by the rein that there was something wrong in the step, and he would have got down and picked out the stone. But this man went on laughing and talking, while with every step the stone became more firmly wedged between my shoe and the frog of my foot. The stone was sharp on the inside and round on the outside, which, as everyone knows, is the most dangerous kind that a horse can pick up, at the same time cutting his foot and making him most liable to stumble and fall.

Whether the man was partly blind, or only very careless, I can't say, but he drove me with that stone in my foot for a good half mile before he saw anything. By that time I was going so lame with the pain that at last he saw it and called out, "Well, here's a go! Why, they have sent us out with a lame horse! What a shame!"

He then chucked the reins and flipped about with the whip, saying, "Now, then, it's no use playing the old soldier with me. There's the journey to go, and it's no use turning lame and lazy."

Just at this time a farmer came riding up on a brown cob. He lifted his hat and pulled up.

"I beg your pardon, sir," he said, "but I think there is something the matter with your horse. He goes very much as if he had a stone in his shoe. If you will allow me, I will look at his feet; these loose scattered stones are confounded dangerous things for the horses."

"He's a hired horse," said my driver. "I don't know what's the matter with him, but it's a great shame to send out a lame beast like this."

The farmer dismounted, and slipped his rein over his arm and at once took up my near foot.

"Bless me, there's a stone! Lame! I should think so!"

At first he tried to dislodge it with his hand, but as it was now very tightly wedged, he drew a stonepick out of his pocket and very carefully, and with some trouble, got it out. Then holding it up, he said, "There, that's the stone your horse had picked up; it is a wonder he did not fall down and break his knees into the bargain!"

"Well, to be sure!" said my driver. "That is a queer thing! I never knew that horses picked up stones before."

"Didn't you?" said the farmer, rather contemptuously. "But they do, though, and the best of them will do it, and can't help it sometimes on such roads as these. And if you don't want to lame your horse, you must look sharp and get them out quickly. This foot is very much bruised," he said, setting it gently down and patting me. "If I might advise, sir, you had better drive him gently for a while. The foot is a good deal hurt, and the lameness will not go off directly."

Then mounting his cob and raising his hat to the lady, he trotted off.

When he was gone my driver began to flop the reins about and whip the harness, by which I understood that I was to go on, which of course I did, glad that the stone was gone, but still in a good deal of pain.

This was the sort of experience we job horses often came in for.

CHAPTER XXIX

Cockneys

THEN THERE IS THE STEAM-ENGINE STYLE OF driving. These drivers were mostly people from towns, who never had a horse of their own, and generally traveled by rail.

They always seemed to think that a horse was something like a steam engine, only smaller. At any rate, they think that if only they pay for it, a horse is bound to go just as far and just as fast and with just as heavy a load as they please. And be the roads heavy and muddy, or dry and good; be they stony or smooth, uphill or downhill, it is all the same—on, on, on, one must go at the same pace, with no relief and no consideration.

These people never think of getting out to walk up a steep hill. Oh, no, they have paid to ride, and ride they will! The horse? Oh, he's used to it! What were horses made for, if not to drag people uphill? Walk! A good joke indeed! And so the whip is plied and the rein is chucked, and often a rough, scolding voice cries out, "Go along, you lazy beast!" And then another slash of the whip, when all the time we are doing our very best to get along, uncomplaining and obedient, though often sorely harassed and down-hearted.

This steam-engine style of driving wears us out faster than any other kind. *I would far rather go twenty miles with a good, considerate driver than I would go ten with some of these; it would take less out of me.*

Another thing—they scarcely ever put on the brake, however steep the downhill may be, and thus bad accidents sometimes happen; or if they do put it on, they often forget to take it off at the bottom of the hill, and more than once I have had to pull halfway up the next hill, with one of the wheels held by the brake, before my driver chose to think about it. And that is a terrible strain on a horse.

Then these cockneys, instead of starting at an easy pace as a gentleman would do, generally set off at full speed from the very stable-yard; and when they want to stop, they first whip us and then pull up so suddenly that we are nearly thrown on our haunches, and our mouths jagged with the bit—they call that pulling up with a dash; and when they turn a corner, they do it as sharply as if there were no right side or wrong side of the road.

I well remember one spring evening I and Rory had been out for the day. (Rory was the horse that mostly went with me when a pair was ordered, and a good honest fellow he was.) We had our own driver, and as he was always considerate and gentle with us, we had a very pleasant day. We were coming home at a good smart pace, about twilight. Our road turned sharp to the left, but as we were close to the hedge on our own side, and there was plenty of room to pass, our driver did not pull us in. As we neared the corner I heard a horse and two wheels coming rapidly down the hill toward us. The hedge was high, and I could see nothing, but the next moment we were upon each other. Happily for me, I was on the side next to the hedge. Rory was on the right side of the pole, and had not even a shaft to protect him. The man who was driving was making straight for the corner, and when he came in sight of us he had no time to pull over to his own side. The whole shock came upon Rory. The gig shaft ran right into his chest, making him stagger back with a cry that I shall never forget. The other horse was thrown upon his haunches, and one shaft broken. It turned out that it was a horse from our own stables, with the high-wheeled gig that the young men were so fond of.

The driver was one of those random, ignorant fellows who don't even know which is their own side of the road, or if they know, don't care. And there was poor Rory with his flesh torn open and bleeding, and the blood streaming down. They said if it had been a little more to one side, it would have killed him; and a good thing for him, poor fellow, if it had.

As it was, it was a long time before the wound healed, and then he was sold for coal carting; *and what that is, up and down those steep hills, only horses know.* Some of the sights I saw there, where a horse had to come downhill with a heavily loaded two-wheel cart behind him, on which no brake could be placed, make me sad even now to think of.

After Rory was disabled, I often went in the carriage with a mare named Peggy, who stood in the next stall to mine. She was a strong, well-made animal, of a bright dun color, beautifully dappled, and with a dark-brown mane and tail. There was no high breeding about her, but she was very pretty, and remarkably sweet-tempered and willing. Still, there was an anxious look about her eye, by which I knew that she had had some trouble. The first time we went out together I thought she had a very odd pace; she seemed to go partly in a trot, partly in a canter, three or four paces, and then to make a little jump forward.

It was very unpleasant for any horse who pulled with her and made me quite fidgety. When we got home, I asked her what made her go in that odd, awkward way.

"Ah," she said in a troubled manner, "I know my paces are very bad, but what can I do? It really is not my fault; it is just because my legs are so short. I stand nearly as high as you, *but your legs are a good three inches longer above your knee than mine,* and of course you can take a much longer step, and go much faster. You see I did not make myself. I wish I could have done so; I would have had long legs then. All my troubles come from my short legs," said Peggy, in a despondent tone.

"But how is it," I said, "when you are so strong and good-tempered and willing?"

"Why, you see," said she, "men will go so fast, and if one can't keep up to other horses, it is nothing but whip, whip, whip, all the time. And so I have had to keep up as I could, and have got into this ugly shuffling pace. It was not always so; when I lived with my first master I always went a good, regular trot, but then he was not in such a hurry. He was a young clergyman in the country, and a good, kind master he was. He had two churches a good way apart, and a great deal of work, but he never scolded or whipped me for not going faster. He was very fond of me. I only wish I was with him now, but he had to leave and go to a large town, and then I was sold to a farmer.

"Some farmers, you know, are capital masters, but I think this one was a low sort of man. He cared nothing about good horses or good driving; he only cared for going fast. I went as fast as I could, but that would not do, and he was always whipping; so I got into this way of making a spring forward to keep up. On market nights he used to stay very late at the inn, and then drive home at a gallop.

"One dark night he was galloping home as usual, when all of a sudden the wheel came against some great heavy thing in the road, and turned the gig over in a minute. He was thrown out and his arm broken, and some of his ribs, I think. At any rate, it was the end of my living with him, and I was not sorry. But you see it will be the same everywhere for me, if men must go so fast. I wish my legs were longer!"

Poor Peggy! I was very sorry for her, and I could not comfort her, for I knew *how hard it was upon slow-paced horses to be put with fast ones; all the whipping comes to their share, and they can't help it.*

She was often used in the phaeton, and was very much liked by some of the ladies because she was so gentle; and some time after this she was sold to two ladies who drove themselves, and wanted a safe, good horse.

I met her several times out in the country, going a good steady pace, and looking as gay and contented as a horse could be. I was very glad to see her, for she deserved a good place.

After she left us, another horse came in her stead. He was young, and had a bad name for shying and starting, by which he had lost a good place. I asked him what made him shy.

"Well, I hardly know," he said. "I was timid when I was young, and was a good deal frightened several times, and if I saw anything strange I used to turn and look at it—you see, *with our blinkers* one can't see or understand what a thing is unless one looks around—and then my master always gave me a whipping, which of course made me start on, and did not make me less afraid. *I think if he would have let me just look at things quietly,* and see that there was nothing to hurt me, it would have been all right, and I should have got used to them. One day an old gentleman was riding with him, and a large piece of white paper rag blew across just on one side of me. I shied and started forward. My master as usual whipped me smartly, but the old man cried out, 'You're wrong! you're wrong! You should never whip a horse for shying; he shies because he is frightened, and you only frighten him more and make the habit worse.' So I suppose all men don't do so. I am sure I don't want to shy for the sake of it. But how should one know what is dangerous and what is not, if one is never allowed to get used to anything? I am never afraid of what I know. Now, I was brought up in a park where there were deer; of course I knew them as well as I did a sheep or a cow, but they are not common, and I know many sensible horses who are frightened at them, and who kick up quite a shindy before they will pass a paddock where there are deer."

I knew what my companion said was true, and I wished that every young horse had as good masters as Farmer Grey and Squire Gordon.

Of course we sometimes came in for good driving here. I remember one morning I was put into the light gig, and taken to a house in Pulteney Street. Two gentlemen came out; the taller of them came round to my head; he looked at the bit and bridle, and just shifted the collar with his hand to see if it fitted comfortably.

"Do you consider this horse wants a curb?" he said to the ostler.

"Well," said the man, "I should say he would go just as well without. He has an uncommon good mouth, and though he has a fine spirit he has no vice; but we generally find people like the curb."

"I don't like it," said the gentleman. "Be so good as to take it off, and put the rein in at the cheek. An easy mouth is a great thing on a long journey, is it not, old fellow?" he said, patting my neck.

Then he took the reins, and they both got up. I can remember now how quietly he turned me round, and then with a light feel of the rein, and drawing the whip gently across my back, we were off.

I arched my neck and set off at my best pace. I found I had someone behind me who knew how a good horse ought to be driven. It seemed like old times again, and made me feel quite gay.

This gentleman took a great liking to me, and after trying me several times with the saddle, he prevailed upon my master to sell me to a friend of his, who wanted a safe, pleasant horse for riding. And so it came to pass that in the summer I was sold to Mr. Barry.

CHAPTER XXX

A Thief

MY NEW MASTER WAS AN UNMARRIED MAN. HE lived at Bath, and was much engaged in business. His doctor advised him to take horse exercise, and for this purpose he bought me. He hired a stable a short distance from his lodgings, and engaged a man named Filcher as groom. My master knew very little about horses, but he treated me well, and I should have had a good and easy place but for circumstances of which he was ignorant. He ordered the best hay with plenty of oats, crushed beans, and bran, with vetches, or rye grass, as the man might think needful. I heard the master give the order, so I knew there was plenty of good food, and I thought I was well off.

For a few days all went on well. I found that my groom understood his business. He kept the stable clean and airy, and he groomed me thoroughly and was never otherwise than gentle. He had been a ostler in one of the great hotels in Bath. He had given that up,

PLATE 5 *Fire!* (Page 67)

PLATE 6 *Can I have your horse?* (Page 78)

PLATE 7 *She chose me for her horse* (Page 102)

PLATE 8 *The morning of Balaclava* (Page 153)

and now cultivated fruit and vegetables for the market, and his wife bred and fattened poultry and rabbits for sale. After a while it seemed to me that my oats came very short; I had the beans, *but bran was mixed with them instead of oats,* of which there were very few; certainly not more than a quarter of what there should have been. In two or three weeks this began to tell upon my strength and spirits. The grass food, though very good, was not the thing to keep up my condition without corn. However, I could not complain, nor make known my wants. So it went on for about two months, and I wondered my master did not see that something was the matter. However, one afternoon he rode out into the country to see a friend of his, a gentleman farmer who lived on the road to Wells.

This gentleman had a very quick eye for horses; and after he had welcomed his friend, he said, casting his eye over me:

"It seems to me, Barry, that your horse does not look so well as he did when you first had him. Has he been well?"

"Yes, I believe so," said my master, "but he is not nearly so lively as he was. My groom tells me that horses are always dull and weak in the autumn, and that I must expect it."

"Autumn, fiddlesticks!" said the farmer. "Why, this is only August; and with your light work and good food he ought not to go down like this, even if it were autumn. How do you feed him?"

My master told him. The other shook his head slowly, and began to feel me over.

"I can't say who eats your corn, my dear fellow, but I am much mistaken if your horse gets it. Have you ridden very fast?"

"No, very gently."

"Then just put your hand here," said he, passing his hand over my neck and shoulder. "He is as warm and damp as a horse just come up from grass. I advise you to look into your stable a little more. I hate to be suspicious, and, thank heaven, I have no cause to be, for I can trust my men, present or absent; *but there are mean scoundrels, wicked enough to rob a dumb beast of his food.* You must look into it." And turning to his man who had come to take me: "Give this horse a right good feed of bruised oats, and don't stint him."

Dumb beasts! Yes, we are, but if I could have spoken I could have told my master where his oats went to. My groom used to come every morning about six o'clock, and with him a little boy, who always had a covered basket with him. He used to go with his father into the harness room where the corn was kept, and I could see them, when the door stood ajar, fill a little bag with oats out of the bin, and then he used to be off.

Five or six mornings after this, just as the boy had left the stable, the door was pushed open and a policeman walked in, holding the child tight by the arm. Another policeman followed, and locked the door on the inside, saying, "Show me the place where your father keeps his rabbits' food."

The boy looked very frightened and began to cry; but there was no escape, and he led the way to the corn bin. Here the policemen found another empty bag like that which was found full of oats in the boy's basket.

Filcher was cleaning my feet at the time, but they soon saw him, and though he blustered a good deal they walked him off to the "lock-up," and his boy with him. I heard afterwards that the boy was not held to be guilty, but the man was sentenced to prison for two months.

CHAPTER XXXI

A Humbug

MY MASTER WAS NOT IMMEDIATELY SUITED, BUT in a few days my new groom came. He was a tall, good-looking fellow enough; but if ever there was a humbug in the shape of a groom, Alfred Smirk was the man. He was very civil to me, and never used me ill; in fact, he did a great deal of stroking and patting, when his master was there to see it. He always brushed my mane and tail with water, and my hoofs with oil, before he brought me to the door, to make me look smart. But as to cleaning my feet, or looking to my shoes, or grooming me thoroughly, he thought no more of that than if I had been a cow. *He left my bit rusty, my saddle damp, and my crupper stiff.*

Alfred Smirk considered himself very handsome; he spent a great deal of time about his hair, whiskers, and necktie before a little looking glass in the harness room. When his master was speaking to him, it was always "Yes, sir; yes, sir," touching his hat at every word, and everyone thought he was a very nice young man, and that Mr. Barry was very fortunate to meet with him. I should say he was the laziest, most conceited fellow I ever came near. Of course it was a great thing not to be ill-used, but then a horse wants more than that. I had a loose box, and might have been very comfortable if he had not been too indolent to clean it out. He never took all the straw away, and *the smell from what lay underneath was very bad;* while the strong vapors that rose up made my eyes smart and inflame, and I did not feel the same appetite for my food.

One day his master came in and said, "Alfred, the stable smells rather strong. Should not you give that stall a good scrub, and throw down plenty of water?"

"Well, sir," he said, touching his cap, "I'll do so if you please, sir; but it is rather dangerous, sir, throwing down water in a horse's box; they are very apt to take cold, sir. I should not like to do him an injury, but I'll do it if you please, sir."

"Well," said the master, "I should not like him to take cold, but I don't like the smell of this stable. Do you think the drains are all right?"

"Well, sir, now you mention it, I think the drain does sometimes send back a smell. There may be something wrong, sir."

"Then send for the bricklayer and have it seen to," said his master.

"Yes, sir, I will."

The bricklayer came, and pulled up a great many bricks, and found nothing amiss, so he put down some lime and charged the master five shillings, and the smell in my box was as bad as ever. But that was not all: *standing as I did on a quantity of moist straw,* my feet grew unhealthy and tender, and the master used to say:

"I don't know what is the matter with this horse. He goes very nimble-footed. I am sometimes afraid he will stumble."

"Yes, sir," said Alfred, "I have noticed the same myself, when I have exercised him."

Now the fact was that he hardly ever did exercise me, and when the master was busy I often stood for days together without stretching my legs at all, and yet being fed just as high as if I were at hard work. This often disordered my health, and made me sometimes heavy and dull, but more often restless and feverish. He never even gave me a meal of green food or a bran mash, which would have cooled me, for he was altogether as ignorant as he was conceited; and then, instead of exercise or change of food, I had to take horse-balls and drafts, which, beside the nuisance of having them poured down my throat, used to make me feel ill and uncomfortable.

One day my feet were so tender that, trotting over some fresh stones with my master on my back, I made two such serious stumbles that, as he came down Lansdown into the city, he stopped at the farrier's and asked him to see what was the matter with me. The man took up my feet one by one and examined them. Then, standing up and dusting his hands one against the other, he said:

"Your horse has got the 'thrush,' and badly too. His feet are very tender; it is fortunate that he has not been down. I wonder your groom has not seen to it before. This is the sort of thing we find in foul stables, where the litter is never properly cleared out. If you will send him here tomorrow, I will attend to the hoof, and I will direct your man how to apply the liniment which I will give him."

The next day I had my feet thoroughly cleansed and stuffed with tow, soaked in some strong lotion, and a very unpleasant business it was.

The farrier ordered all the litter to be taken out of my box day by day, and the floor kept very clean. Then I was to have bran mashes, a little green food, and not so much corn, till my feet were well again. With this treatment I soon regained my spirits, but Mr. Barry was so much disgusted at being twice deceived by his grooms that he determined to give up keeping a horse, and to hire when he wanted one. I was therefore kept till my feet were quite sound and was then sold again.

Part Three

CHAPTER XXXII

A Horse Fair

NO DOUBT A HORSE FAIR IS A VERY AMUSING PLACE to those who have nothing to lose. At any rate, there is plenty to see.

Long strings of young horses out of the country, fresh from the marshes; and droves of shaggy little Welsh ponies, no higher than Merrylegs; and hundreds of cart horses of all sorts, some of them with their long tails braided up and tied with scarlet cord; and a good many like myself, handsome and highbred, but fallen into the middle class, through some accident or blemish, un-soundness of wind, or some other complaint. There were some splendid animals quite in their prime and fit for anything. They were throwing out their legs and showing off their paces in high style, as they were trotted out with a leading-rein, the groom running by the side. But round in the background there were a number of poor things, sadly broken down with hard work, with their knees knuckling over and their hind legs swinging out at every step. And there were some very dejected-looking old horses, with the underlip hanging down and the ears lying back heavily, as if there was no more pleasure in life, and no more hope. There were some so thin you might see all their ribs, and some with old sores on their backs and hips. These were sad sights for a horse to look upon who knows not but he may come to the same state.

There was a great deal of bargaining, of running up and beating down; and, if a horse may speak his mind so far as he understands, I should say *there were more lies told and more trickery at that horse fair than a clever man could give an account of.* I was put with two or three other strong, useful-looking horses, and a good many people came to look at us. The gentlemen always turned from me when they saw my broken knees, though the man who had me swore it was only a slip in the stall.

The first thing was to pull my mouth open, then to look at my eyes, then feel all the way down my legs, and give me a hard feel of the skin and flesh, and then try my paces. It was wonderful what a difference there was in the way these things were done. Some did it in a rough, offhand way, as if one was only a piece of wood; while others would take their hands gently over one's body, with a pat now and then, as much as to say, "By your leave." Of course I judged a good deal of the buyers by their manners to myself.

There was one man, I thought, if he would buy me, I should be happy. He was not a gentleman, nor yet one of the loud, flashy sort that called themselves so. He was rather a small man, but well made and quick in all his motions. I knew in a moment by the way he handled me that he was used to horses. He spoke gently, and his gray eye had a kindly, cheery look in it. It may seem strange to say—but it is true all the same—that the clean, fresh smell there was about him made me take to him: *no smell of old beer and tobacco,* which I hated, but a fresh smell as if he had come out of a hayloft. He offered twenty-three pounds for me, but that was refused, and he walked away. I looked after him, but he was gone, and a very hard-looking, loud-voiced man came. I was dreadfully afraid he would have me, but he walked off. One or two more came who did not mean business. Then the hard-faced man came back again and offered twenty-three pounds. A very close bargain was being driven, for my salesman began to think he should not get all he asked, and must come down; but just then the gray-eyed man came back again. I could not help reaching out my head toward him. He stroked my face kindly.

"Well, old chap," he said, "I think we should suit each other. I'll give twenty-four for him."

"Say twenty-five and you shall have him."

"Twenty-four ten," said my friend, in a very decided tone, "and not another sixpence—yes or no?"

"Done," said the salesman, "and you may depend upon it there's a monstrous deal of quality in that horse, and if you want him for cab work, he's a bargain."

The money was paid on the spot, and my new master took my halter, and led me out of the fair to an inn, where he had a saddle and bridle ready. He gave me a good feed of oats and stood by while I ate it, talking to himself and talking to me. Half an hour after, we were on our way to London, through pleasant lanes and country roads, until we came into the great London thoroughfare, on which we traveled steadily, till in the twilight we reached the great city. The gas lamps were already lighted. There were streets to the right, and streets to the left, and streets crossing each other for mile upon mile. I thought we should never come to the end of them. At last, in passing through one, we came to a long cabstand, where my rider called out in a cheery voice, "Goodnight, Governor!"

"Halloo!" cried a voice. "Have you got a good one?"

"I think so," replied my owner.

"I wish you luck with him."

"Thank ye, Governor." And he rode on. We soon turned up one of the side streets, and about halfway up that we turned into a very narrow street, with rather poor-looking houses on one side, and what seemed to be coach-houses and stables on the other.

My owner pulled up at one of the houses and whistled. The door flew open, and a young woman, followed by a little girl and boy, ran out. There was a very lively greeting as my rider dismounted.

"Now then, Harry, my boy, open the gates, and mother will bring us the lantern."

The next minute they were all standing round me in a small stable yard.

"Is he gentle, father?"

"Yes, Dolly, as gentle as your own kitten. Come and pat him."

At once the little hand was patting all over my shoulder without fear. How good it felt!

"Let me get him a bran mash while you rub him down," said the mother.

"Do, Polly, it's just what he wants, and I know you've got a beautiful mash ready for me."

"Sausage dumpling and apple turnover!" shouted the boy, which set them all laughing. I was led into a comfortable, clean-smelling stall, with plenty of dry straw, and after a capital supper I lay down, thinking I was to be happy.

CHAPTER XXXIII

A London Cab Horse

MY NEW MASTER'S NAME WAS JEREMIAH BARKER, but as everyone called him Jerry, I shall do the same. Polly, his wife, was just as good a match as a man could have. She was a plump, trim, tidy little woman, with smooth, dark hair, dark eyes, and a merry little mouth. The boy was nearly twelve years old, a tall, frank, good-tempered lad; and Little Dorothy (Dolly, they called her) was her mother over again, at eight years old. They were all wonderfully fond of each other. I never knew such a happy, merry family before or since. Jerry had a cab of his own, and two horses, which he drove and attended to himself. His other horse was a tall, white, rather large-boned animal called Captain. He was old now, but when he was young, he must have been splendid. He had still a proud way of holding his head and arching his neck; in fact, he was a high-bred, fine-mannered, noble old horse, every inch of him. He told me that in his early youth he went to the Crimean

War. He belonged to an officer in the cavalry and used to lead the regiment. I will tell more of that hereafter.

The next morning, when I was well groomed, Polly and Dolly came into the yard to see me and make friends. Harry had been helping his father since the early morning, and had stated his opinion that I should turn out "a regular brick." Polly brought me a slice of apple, and Dolly a piece of bread, and made as much of me as if I had been the "Black Beauty" of olden time. It was a great treat to be petted again and talked to in a gentle voice, and I let them see as well as I could that I wished to be friendly. Polly thought I was very handsome, and a great deal too good for a cab, if it was not for the broken knees.

"Of course there's no one to tell us whose fault that was," said Jerry, "and as long as I don't know, I shall give him the benefit of the doubt, for a firmer, neater stepper I never rode. We'll call him 'Jack,' after the old one—shall we, Polly?"

"Do," she said, "for I like to keep a good name going."

Captain went out in the cab all the morning. Harry came in after school to feed me and give me water. In the afternoon I was put into the cab. Jerry took as much pains to see if the collar and bridle fitted comfortably as if he had been John Manly over again. When the crupper was let out a hole or two, it all fitted well. There was no check-rein, no curb, nothing but a plain ring snaffle. What a blessing that was!

After driving through the side street we came to the large cabstand where Jerry had said "Good-night." On one side of this wide street were high houses with wonderful shop fronts, and on the other was an old church and churchyard, surrounded by iron palisades. Alongside these iron rails a number of cabs were drawn up, waiting for passengers. Bits of hay were lying about on the ground. Some of the men were standing together talking; some were sitting on their boxes reading the newspapers; and one or two were feeding their horses with bits of hay and a drink of water. We pulled up in the rank at the back of the last cab. Two or three men came round and began to look at me and pass their remarks. "Very good for a funeral," said one.

"Too smart-looking," said another, shaking his head in a wise way. "You'll find out something wrong one of these fine mornings."

"Well," said Jerry pleasantly, "I suppose I need not find it out till it finds me out, eh? And if so, I'll keep up my spirits a little longer."

Then came up a broad-faced man dressed in a great gray coat with great gray capes and great white buttons, a gray hat, and a blue comforter loosely tied round his neck; his hair was gray too, but he was a jolly-looking fellow, and the other men made way for him. He looked me all over, as if he had been going to buy me, and then straightening himself up with a grunt, he said, "He's the right sort for you, Jerry. I don't care what you gave for him, he'll be worth it." Thus my character was established on the stand.

This man's name was Grant, but he was called "Gray Grant," or "Governor Grant." He had been the longest on that stand of any of the men, and he took it upon himself to settle matters and stop disputes. He was generally a good-humored, sensible man; but if his temper was a little out, as it was sometimes when he had drunk too much, nobody liked to come too near his fist, for he could deal a very heavy blow.

The first week of my life as a cab horse was very trying. I had never been used to London, and the noise, the hurry, the crowds of horses, carts, and carriages that I had to make my way through made me feel anxious and harassed. But I soon found that I could perfectly trust my driver, and then I made myself easy, and got used to it.

Jerry was as good a driver as I had ever known, and what was better, *he took as much thought for his horses as he did for himself.* He soon found out that I was willing to work and do my best; and he never laid the whip on me, unless it was gently drawing the end of it over my back when I was to go on. But generally I knew this well by the way in which he took up the reins, and I believe his whip was more often stuck up by his side than in his hand.

In a short time I and my master understood each other as well as horse and man can do. In the stable, too, he did all that he could for our comfort. The stalls were the old-fashioned style, too much on the slope; but he had two movable bars fixed across the back of our stalls, so that at night, and when we were resting, he just took off our halters and put up the bars, and thus we could turn about and stand whichever way we pleased, which is a comfort.

Jerry kept us very clean, and gave us as much change of food as he could, and always plenty of it; and not only that, but he always gave us plenty of clean, fresh water, which he allowed to stand by us both day and night, *except of course when we came in warm.* Some people say that a horse ought not to drink all he likes, but I know if we are allowed to drink when we want it we drink only a little at a time, and it does us a great deal more good than swallowing down half a bucketful at a time, because we have been left without till we are thirsty and miserable. Some grooms will go home to their beer and leave us for hours with our dry hay and oats and nothing to moisten them. Then of course we gulp down too much at once, which helps to spoil our breathing and sometimes chills our stomachs.

But the best thing that we had was our Sundays for rest! We worked so hard in the week that I do not think we could have kept up to it but for that day. Besides, we had time to enjoy each other's company. On these days I learned my companion's history.

CHAPTER XXXIV

An Old War Horse

CAPTAIN HAD BEEN BROKEN IN AND TRAINED FOR an army horse. His first owner was an officer of cavalry going out to the Crimean War. He said he quite enjoyed the training with all the other horses, trotting together, turning together, to the right hand or to the left, halting at the word of command, or dashing forward at full speed at the sound of the trumpet, or signal of the officer. He was, when young, a dark, dappled iron gray, and considered very handsome. His master, a young, high-spirited gentleman, was very fond of him, and treated him from the first with the greatest care and kindness. He told me he thought the life of an army horse was very pleasant, but when it came to being sent abroad, over the sea in a great ship, he almost changed his mind.

"That part of it," said he, "was dreadful! Of course we could not walk off the land into the ship, so they were obliged to put strong straps under our bodies, and then we were lifted off our legs in spite of our struggles, and were swung through the air over the water, to the deck of the great vessel. There we were placed in small, close stalls, and never for a long time saw the sky, or were able to stretch our legs. The ship sometimes rolled about in high winds, and we were knocked about, and felt bad enough. However, at last it came to an end, and we were hauled up, and swung over again to the land. We were very glad, and snorted and neighed for joy when we once more felt firm ground under our feet.

"We soon found that the country we had come to was very different from our own and that we had many hardships to endure besides the fighting; but many of the men were so fond of their horses that they did everything they could to make them comfortable, in spite of snow, wet, and all things out of order."

"But what about the fighting?" said I. "Was not that worse than anything else?"

"Well," said he, "I hardly know; we always liked to hear the trumpet sound, and to be called out, and were impatient to start off, though sometimes we had to stand for hours, waiting for the word of command. And when the word was given, we used to spring forward as gaily and eagerly as if there were no cannonballs, bayonets, or bullets. I believe so long as we felt our rider in the saddle, and his hand steady on the bridle, not one of us gave way to fear, not even when the terrible bombshells whirled through the air and burst into a thousand pieces.

"I, with my noble master, went into many actions together without a wound. And though I saw horses shot down with bullets, pierced through with lances, and gashed with fearful saber-cuts; though we left them dead on the field, or dying in the agony of their wounds, I don't think I feared for myself. My master's cheery voice, as he encouraged his men, made me feel as if he and I could not be killed. I had such perfect trust in him that while he was guiding me I was ready to charge up to the very cannon's mouth. I saw many brave men cut down, many fall mortally wounded from their saddles. I had heard the cries and groans of the dying, I had cantered over ground slippery with blood, and frequently had to turn aside to avoid trampling on wounded man or horse, but, until one dreadful day, I had never felt terror. That day I shall never forget."

Here old Captain paused for a while and drew a long breath. I waited, and he went on.

"It was one autumn morning, and as usual, an hour before daybreak our cavalry had turned out, ready caparisoned for the day's work, whether it might be fighting or waiting. The men stood by their horses waiting, ready for orders. As the light increased there seemed to be some excitement among the officers. And before the day was well begun, we heard the firing of enemy guns.

"Then one of the officers rode up and gave the word for the men to mount, and in a second every man was in his saddle, and every horse stood expecting the touch of the rein, or the pressure of his rider's heels, all animated, all eager. But still we had been trained so well, that, except by the champing of our bits, and the restive tossing of our heads from time to time, it could not be said that we stirred.

"My dear master and I were at the head of the line, and as all sat motionless and watchful he took a little stray lock of my mane which had turned over on the wrong side, laid it over on the right, and smoothed it down with his hand. Then, patting my neck, he said, 'We shall have a day of it today, Bayard, my beauty, but we'll do our duty as we have done.' He stroked my neck that morning, more, I think, than he had ever done before, quietly on and on, as if he were thinking of something else. I loved to feel his hand on my neck, and arched my chest proudly and happily; but I stood very still, for I knew all his moods, and when he liked me to be quiet, and when gay.

"I cannot tell all that happened on that day, but I will tell of the last charge that we made together. It was across a valley right in front of the enemy's cannon. By this time we were all used to the roar of heavy guns, the rattle of musket fire, and the flying of shot near us; but never had I been under such a fire as we rode through on that day. From the right, from the left, and from the front, shot and shell poured in upon us. Many a brave man went down, many a horse fell, flinging his rider to the earth. Many a horse without a rider ran wildly out of the ranks, then, terrified at being alone, with no hand to guide him, came pressing in among his companions, to gallop with them to the charge.

"Fearful as it was, no one stopped, no one turned back. Every moment the ranks were thinned, but as our comrades fell, we closed in to keep them together; and instead of being shaken or staggered in our pace, our gallop became faster as we neared the cannon, all clouded in white smoke, while the red fire flashed through it.

"My master, my dear master, was cheering on his comrades with his right arm raised on high, when one of the balls, whizzing close to my head, struck him. I felt him stagger with the shock, though he uttered no cry. I tried to check my speed, but the sword dropped from his right hand, the rein fell loose from the left, and sinking backward from the saddle, he fell to the earth. The other riders swept past us, and by the force of their charge I was driven from the spot where he fell.

"I wanted to keep my place by his side, and not leave him under that rush of horses' feet, but it was in vain. And now, without a master or a friend, I was alone on that great slaughter ground. Then fear took hold of me, and I trembled as I had never trembled before; and I, too, as I had seen other horses do, tried to join in the ranks and gallop with them, but I was beaten off by the swords of the soldiers. Just then, a soldier whose horse had been killed under him caught at my bridle and mounted me, and with this new master I was again going forward.

"But our gallant company was cruelly overpowered, and those who remained alive after the fierce fight for the guns came galloping back over the same ground. Some of the horses had been so badly wounded that they could scarcely move from the loss of blood. Other noble creatures were trying on three legs to drag themselves along, and others were struggling to rise on their forefeet when their hind legs had been shattered by shot. Their groans were piteous to hear, and the beseeching look in their eyes as those who escaped passed by and left them to their fate, I shall never forget. After the battle the wounded men were brought in and the dead were buried."

"And what about the wounded horses?" I said. "Were they left to die?"

"No, the army farriers went over the field with their pistols and shot all that were ruined. Some that had only slight wounds were brought back and attended to, but the greater part of the noble, willing creatures that went out that morning never came back! In our stables there was only about one in four that returned.

"I never saw my dear master again. I believe he fell dead from the saddle. I never loved any other master so well. I went into many other engagements, but was only once wounded, and then not seriously. And when the war was over, I came back to England, as sound and strong as when I went out."

I said, "I have heard people talk about war as if it was a very fine thing."

"Ah!" said he. "I should think they never saw it. No doubt it is very fine when there is no enemy, when it is just exercise and parade, and sham fight. Yes, it is very fine then; but when thousands of good brave men and horses are killed or crippled for life, it has a very different look."

"Do you know what they fought about?" said I.

"No," he said, "that is more than a horse can understand, but the enemy must have been awfully wicked people, if it was right to go all that way over the sea on purpose to kill them."

CHAPTER XXXV

Jerry Barker

I NEVER KNEW A BETTER MAN THAN MY NEW MASTER. He was kind and good, and as strong for the right as John Manly, and so good-tempered and merry that very few people could pick a quarrel with him. He was very fond of making little songs, and singing them to himself. One he was very fond of was this:

"Come, father and mother,
And sister and brother,
Come, all of you, turn to
And help one another."

And so they did. Harry was as clever at stable work as a much older boy, and always wanted to do what he could. Then Polly and Dolly used to come in the morning to help with the cab—to brush and beat the cushions and rub the glass while Jerry was giving us a cleaning in the yard and Harry was rubbing the harness. There used to be a great deal of laughing and fun between them, and it put Captain and me in much better spirits than if we had heard scolding and hard words. They were always early in the morning, for Jerry would say:

> "If you in the morning
>   Throw minutes away,
> You can't pick them up
>   In the course of the day;
> You may hurry and scurry,
>   And flurry and worry,
> You've lost them forever,
>   Forever and aye."

He could not bear any careless loitering and waste of time, and nothing was so near making him angry as to find people who were always late, wanting a cab horse to be driven hard, to make up for their idleness.

One day, two wild-looking young men came out of a tavern close by the stand, and called Jerry.

"Here, cabby! Look sharp, we are rather late. Put on the steam, will you, and take us to the Victoria in time for the one o'clock train? You shall have a shilling extra."

"I will take you at the regular pace, gentlemen. Shillings don't pay for putting on steam like that."

Larry's cab was standing next to ours. He flung open the door and said, "I'm your man, gentlemen! Take my cab, my horse will get you there all right"; and as he shut them in, with a wink toward

Jerry, said, "It's against his conscience to go beyond a jog trot." Then, slashing his jaded horse, he set off as hard as he could. Jerry patted me on the neck. "No, Jack, a shilling would not pay for that sort of thing, would it, old boy?"

Although Jerry was determinedly set against hard driving to please careless people, he always went a good fair pace, and was not against putting on the steam, as he said, if only he knew *why*.

I well remember one morning, as we were on the stand waiting for a fare, that a young man, carrying a heavy portmanteau, trod on a piece of orange peel which lay on the pavement, and fell down with great force.

Jerry was the first to run and lift him up. He seemed much stunned, and as they led him into a shop, he walked as if he were in great pain. Jerry, of course, came back to the stand, but in about ten minutes one of the shopmen called him, so we drew up to the pavement.

"Can you take me to the South-Eastern Railway?" said the young man. "This unlucky fall has made me late, I fear; but it is of great importance that I should not lose the twelve o'clock train. I should be most thankful if you could get me there in time, and will gladly pay you an extra fare."

"I'll do my very best," said Jerry heartily, "if you think you are well enough, sir," for he looked dreadfully white and ill.

"I *must* go," he said earnestly. "Please open the door, and let us lose no time."

The next minute Jerry was on the box, with a cheery chirrup to me, and a twitch of the rein that I well understood.

"Now, then, Jack, my boy," said he, "spin along; we'll show them how we can get over the ground, if we only know why."

It is always difficult to drive fast in the city in the middle of the day, when the streets are full of traffic, but we did what could be done; and when a good driver and a good horse, who understand each other, are of one mind, it is wonderful what they can do. I had a very good mouth—that is, I could be guided by the slightest touch of the rein. And that is a great thing in London, amongst carriages, omnibuses, carts, vans, trucks, cabs, and great wagons creeping along at a walking pace; some going one way, some another, some going slowly, others wanting to pass them; omnibuses stopping short every few minutes to take up a passenger, obliging the horse that is coming up behind to pull up too, or to pass, and get before them. Perhaps you try to pass, but just then something else comes dashing in through the narrow opening, and you have to keep in behind the omnibus again; presently you think you see a chance and manage to get to the front, getting so near the wheels on each side that half an inch nearer and they would scrape. Well—you get along for a bit, but soon find yourself in a long train of carts and carriages all obliged to go at a walk. Perhaps you come to a regular block-up, and have to stand still for minutes together, till something clears out into a side street, or the policeman interferes; you have to be ready for any chance—to dash forward if there be an opening, and be quick as a rat dog to see if there be room, and if there be time, lest you get your own wheels locked or smashed, or the shaft of some other vehicle run into your chest or shoulder. All this is what you have to be ready for. If you want to get through London fast in the middle of the day, it wants a deal of practice.

Jerry and I were used to it, and no one could beat us at getting through when we were set upon it. I was quick and bold and could always trust my driver; Jerry was quick, and patient at the same time, and could trust his horse, which was a great thing, too. He very seldom used the whip; I knew by his voice, and his click, click, when he wanted to get on fast, and by the rein where I was to go; so there was no need for whipping. But I must go back to my story.

The streets were very full that day, but we got on pretty well as far as the bottom of Cheapside, where there was a block for three or four minutes. The young man put his head out and said anxiously, "I think I had better get out and walk. I shall never get there if this goes on."

"I'll do all that can be done, sir," said Jerry. "I think we shall be in time. This block-up cannot last much longer, and your luggage is very heavy for you to carry, sir."

Just then the cart in front of us began to move on, and then we had a good turn. In and out, in and out we went, as fast as horse-flesh could do it, and for a wonder had a good clear time on London Bridge, for there was a whole train of cabs and carriages, all going our way at a quick trot—perhaps wanting to catch that very train; at any rate, we whirled into the station, with many more, just as the great clock pointed to eight minutes to twelve o'clock.

"Thank God! We are in time," said the young man, "and thank you, too, my friend, and your good horse. You have saved me more than money can ever pay for; take this extra half crown."

"No, sir, no, thank you all the same; so glad we hit the time, sir; but don't stay now, sir, the bell is ringing. Here, porter! Take this gentleman's luggage—Dover line—twelve o'clock train—that's it." And without waiting for another word, Jerry wheeled me round to make room for the other cabs that were dashing up at the last minute, and drew up on one side till the crush was passed.

"So glad!" he said. "So glad! Poor young fellow! I wonder what it was that made him so anxious?"

Jerry often talked to himself quite loud enough for me to hear, when we were not moving.

On Jerry's return to the rank, there was a good deal of laughing and chaffing at him for driving hard to the train for an extra fare, as they said, all against his principles, and they wanted to know how much he had pocketed.

"A good deal more than I generally get," said he, nodding slyly. "What he gave me will keep me in little comforts for several days."

"Gammon!" said one.

"He's a humbug," said another, "preaching to us, and then doing the same himself."

"Look here, mates," said Jerry, "the gentleman offered me half-a-crown extra, but I didn't take it; 'twas quite pay enough for me to see how glad he was to catch that train; and if Jack and I choose to have a quick run now and then, to please ourselves, that's our business and not yours."

"Well," said Larry, "*you'll* never be a rich man."

"Most likely not," said Jerry, "but I don't know that I shall be the less happy for that. I have heard the Commandments read a great many times, and I never noticed that any of them said, 'Thou shalt be rich.' And there are a good many curious things said in the New Testament about rich men that I think would make me feel rather queer if I was one of them."

"If you ever do get rich," said Governor Gray, looking over his shoulder across the top of his cab, "you'll deserve it, Jerry, and you won't find a curse come with your wealth. As for you, Larry, you'll die poor; you spend too much in whipcord."

"Well," said Larry, "what is a fellow to do if his horse won't go without it?"

"You never take the trouble to see if he will go without it; your whip is always going as if you had the St. Vitus dance in your arm; and if it does not wear you out, it wears your horse out. You know you are always changing your horses, and why? Because you never give them any peace or encouragement."

"Well, I have not had good luck," said Larry, "that's where it is."

"And you never will," said the Governor. "Good Luck is rather particular who she drives with, and mostly prefers those who have got common sense and a good heart; at least, that is my experience."

Governor Gray turned around again to his newspaper, and the other men went to their cabs.

CHAPTER XXXVI

The Sunday Cab

ONE MORNING, AS JERRY HAD JUST PUT ME INTO the shafts and was fastening the traces, a gentleman walked into the yard. "Your servant, sir," said Jerry.

"Good morning, Mr. Barker," said the gentleman. "I should be glad to make some arrangements with you for taking Mrs. Briggs regularly to church on Sunday mornings. We go to the New Church now, and that is rather further than she can walk."

"Thank you, sir," said Jerry, "but I have only taken out a six-day license, and therefore I could not take a fare on a Sunday; it would be illegal."

"Oh!" said the other. "I did not know yours was a six-day cab, but of course it would be very easy to alter your license. I would see that you did not lose by it. The fact is, Mrs. Briggs very much prefers you to drive her."

"I should be glad to oblige the lady, sir, but I had a seven-day license once, and the work was too hard for me, *and too hard for my horses.* Year in and year out, not a day's rest, and never a Sunday with my wife and children; and never able to go to a place of worship, which I had always been used to do before I took the driving box. So for the last five years I have only taken a six-day license, and I find it better all the way round."

"Well, of course," replied Mr. Briggs, "it is very proper that every person should have rest, and be able to go to church on Sundays, but I should have thought you would not have minded such a short distance for the horse, and only once a day. You would have all the afternoon and evening for yourself, and we are very good customers, you know."

"Yes, sir, that is true, and I am grateful for all favors, I am sure, and anything that I could do to oblige you, or the lady, I should be proud and happy to do; but I can't give up my Sundays, sir, indeed I can't. I read that God made man, and *He made horses* and all the other beasts, and as soon as He had made them He made a day of rest, and bade *that all should rest one day in seven;* and I think, sir, He must have known what was good for them, and I am sure it is good for me; I am stronger and healthier altogether, now that I have a day of rest. The horses are fresh, too, and do not wear out nearly so fast. The six-day drivers all tell me the same, and I have laid by more money in the Savings' Bank than ever I did before; and as for the wife and children, sir, why, heart alive! They would not go back to the seven days for all they could see."

"Oh, very well," said the gentleman. "Don't trouble yourself, Mr. Barker, any further. I will inquire somewhere else." And he walked away.

"Well," says Jerry to me, "we can't help it, Jack, old boy, we must have our Sundays.

"Polly!" he shouted. "Polly! Come here."

She was there in a minute.

"What is it all about, Jerry?"

"Why, my dear, Mr. Briggs wants me to take Mrs. Briggs to church every Sunday morning. I say, 'I have only a six-day license.' He says, 'Get a seven-day license, and I'll make it worth your while.' And you know, Polly, they are very good customers to us. Mrs. Briggs often goes out shopping for hours, or making calls, and then she pays down fair and honorable like a lady; there's no beating down, or making three hours into two hours and a half, as some folks do. And it is easy work for the horses, not like tearing along to catch trains for people that are always a quarter of an hour too late. And if I don't oblige her in this matter, it is very likely we shall lose them altogether. What do you say, little woman?"

"I say, Jerry," says she, speaking very slowly, "I say, if Mrs. Briggs would give you a sovereign every Sunday morning I would not have you a seven-day cabman again. We have known what it was to have no Sundays, and now we know what it is to call them our own. Thank God, you earn enough to keep us, though it is sometimes close work to pay for all the oats and hay, the license, and the rent besides. But Harry will soon be earning something, and I would rather struggle on harder than we do than go back to those horrid times when you hardly had a minute to look at your own children, and we never could go to a place of worship together, or have a quiet, happy day. God forbid that we should ever turn back to those times. That's what I say, Jerry."

"And that is just what I told Mr. Briggs, my dear," said Jerry, "and what I mean to stick to; So don't go and fret yourself, Polly (for she had begun to cry); I would not go back to the old times if I earned twice as much, so that is settled, little woman; cheer up. Now, I'll be off to the stand."

Three weeks had passed away after this conversation, and no order had come from Mrs. Briggs, so there was nothing but taking jobs from the stand. Jerry took it to heart a good deal, for, of course, the work was harder for horse and man; but Polly would always cheer him up and say, "Never mind, father, never mind.

"Do your best
And leave the rest;
'Twill all come right
Some day or night."

It soon became known that Jerry had lost his best customer, and for what reason; most of the men said he was a fool, but two or three took his part.

"If workingmen don't stick to their Sunday," said Truman, "they'll soon have none left; *it is every man's right and every beast's right. By God's law we have a day of rest, and by the law of England we have a day of rest; and I say we ought to hold to the rights these laws give us, and keep them for our children.*"

"All very well for you religious chaps to talk so," said Larry, "but I'll turn a shilling when I can. I don't believe in religion, for I don't see that your religious people are any better than the rest."

"If they are not better," put in Jerry, "it is because they are *not* religious. You might as well say that our country's laws are not good because some people break them. If a man gives way to his temper, and speaks evil of his neighbor, and does not pay his debts, he is *not* religious. I don't care how much he goes to church. If some men are shams and humbugs, that does not make religion untrue. Real religion is the best and the truest thing in the world, and the only thing that can make a man really happy, or make the world better."

"If religion was good for anything," said Jones, "it would prevent your religious people from making us work on Sundays, as you know many of them do, and that's why I say religion is nothing but a sham; why, if it was not for the church- and chapel-goers, it would be hardly worthwhile our coming out on a Sunday; but they have their privileges, as they call them, and I go without. I shall expect them to answer for my soul if I can't get a chance of saving it."

Several of the men applauded this, till Jerry said:

"That may sound well enough, but it won't do; every man must look after his own soul. You can't lay it at another man's door like a foundling, and expect him to take care of it. Don't you see, if you are always sitting on your box waiting for a fare, they will say, 'If we don't take him, someone else will, and he does not look for any Sunday.' Of course they don't go to the bottom of it, or they would see if they never came for a cab it would be no use your standing there. But people don't always like to go to the bottom of things; it may not be convenient to do it. But if you Sunday drivers would strike for a day of rest, the thing would be done."

"And what would all the good people do if they could not get to their favorite preachers?" said Larry.

" 'Tis not for me to lay down plans for other people," said Jerry, "but if they can't walk so far, they can go to what is nearer; and if it should rain, they can put on their mackintoshes as they do on a weekday. If a thing is right, it *can* be done, and if it is wrong, it *can be done without;* and a good man will find a way. And that is as true for us cabmen as it is for the churchgoers."

CHAPTER XXXVII

The Golden Rule

TWO OR THREE WEEKS AFTER THIS, AS WE CAME into the yard rather late in the evening, Polly came running across the road with the lantern (she always brought it to him if it was not very wet).

"It has all come right, Jerry; Mrs. Briggs sent her servant this afternoon to ask you to take her out tomorrow at eleven o'clock. I said, Yes, I thought so, but we supposed she employed someone else now."

"'Well,' he said, 'the real fact is, master was put out because Mr. Barker refused to come on Sundays, and he has been trying other cabs, but there's something wrong with them all; some drive too fast, and some too slow, and the mistress says there is not one of them so nice and clean as yours, and nothing will suit her but Mr. Barker's cab again.'"

Polly was almost out of breath, and Jerry broke out into a merry laugh.

"*'Twill all come right some day or night.'* You were right, my dear; you generally are. Run in and get the supper, and I'll have Jack's harness off and make him snug and happy in no time."

After this, Mrs. Briggs wanted Jerry's cab quite as often as before—never, however, on a Sunday. But there came a day when he had Sunday work, and this was how it happened. We had all come home on the Saturday night very tired, and very glad to think that the next day would be all rest, but so it was not to be.

On Sunday morning Jerry was cleaning me in the yard, when Polly stepped up to him, looking very full of something. "What is it?" said Jerry.

"Well, my dear," she said, "poor Dinah Brown has just had a letter brought to say that her mother is dangerously ill, and that she must go directly if she wishes to see her alive. The place is more than ten miles away from here, out in the country, and she says if she takes the train she would still have four miles to walk. And so weak as she is, and the baby only four weeks old, of course that would be impossible, and she wants to know if you would take her in your cab, and she promises to pay you faithfully, as she can get the money."

"Tut, tut, we'll see about that. It was not the money I was thinking about, but of losing our Sunday; the horses are tired, and I am tired too—that's where it pinches."

"It pinches all round, for that matter," said Polly, "for it's only half Sunday without you, but you know we should do to other people as we should like they should do to us; and I know very well what I should like if my mother was dying. And, Jerry, dear, I am sure it won't break the Sabbath, for if pulling a poor beast or donkey out of a pit would not spoil it, I am quite sure taking poor Dinah would not do it."

"Why, Polly, you are as good as the minister, and so, as I've had my Sunday morning sermon early today, you may go and tell Dinah that I'll be ready for her as the clock strikes ten. But stop—just step around to Butcher Braydon's with my compliments, and ask him if he would lend me his light trap; I know he never uses it on the Sunday, *and it would make a wonderful difference to the horse.*"

Away she went, and soon returned, saying that he could have the trap and welcome.

"All right," said he, "now put me up a bit of bread and cheese, and I'll be back in the afternoon as soon as I can."

"And I'll have the meat-pie ready for an early tea instead of for dinner," said Polly, and away she went, while he made his preparations to the tune of "Polly's the woman and no mistake," of which tune he was very fond.

I was selected for the journey, and at ten o'clock we started, in a light, high-wheeled gig, which ran so easily that after the four-wheeled cab it seemed like nothing.

It was a fine May day, and as soon as we were out of the town, the sweet air, the smell of the fresh grass, and the soft country roads were as pleasant as they used to be in the old times, and I soon began to feel quite fresh.

Dinah's family lived in a small farmhouse, up a green lane, close by a meadow with some fine shady trees; there were two cows feeding in it. A young man asked Jerry to bring his trap into the meadow, and he would tie me up in the cowshed; he wished he had a better stable to offer.

"If your cows would not be offended," said Jerry, "there is nothing my horse would like so well as to have an hour or two in your beautiful meadow. He's quiet, and it would be a rare treat for him."

"Do, and welcome," said the young man. "The best we have is at your service for your kindness to my sister. We shall be having some dinner in an hour, and I hope you'll come in, though with mother so ill we are all out of sorts in the house."

Jerry thanked him kindly, but said as he had some dinner with him, there was nothing he should like so well as walking about in the meadow.

When my harness was taken off, I did not know what I should do first—whether to eat the grass, or roll over on my back, or lie down and rest, or have a gallop across the meadow out of sheer spirits at being free; and I did all by turns. Jerry seemed to be quite as happy as I was; he sat down by a bank under a shady tree, and listened to the birds, then he sang to himself, and read out of the little brown book he is so fond of, then wandered round the meadow and down by a little brook, where he picked the flowers and the hawthorn, and tied them up with long sprays of ivy. Then he gave me a good feed of the oats which he had brought with him; but the time seemed all too short—I had not been in a field since I left poor Ginger at Earlshall.

We came home gently, and Jerry's first words were, as we came into the yard, "Well, Polly, I have not lost my Sunday after all, for the birds were singing hymns in every bush, and I joined in the service; and as for Jack, he was like a young colt."

When he handed Dolly the flowers, she jumped about for joy.

CHAPTER XXXVIII

Dolly and a Real Gentleman

THE WINTER CAME IN EARLY, WITH A GREAT DEAL of cold and wet. There was snow, or sleet, or rain, almost every day for weeks, changing only for keen driving winds, or sharp frosts. The horses all felt it very much. When it is a dry cold, a couple of good, thick rugs will keep the warmth in us; but when it is soaking rain, they soon get wet through and are no good. Some of the drivers had a waterproof cover to throw over, which was a fine thing; but some of the men were so poor that they could not protect either themselves or their horses, and many of them suffered very much that winter. When we horses worked half the day we went to our dry stables, and could rest, while they had to sit on their boxes, sometimes staying out as late as one or two o'clock in the morning, if they had a party to wait for.

When the streets were slippery with frost or snow, that was the worst of all for us horses. One mile of such traveling with a weight to draw, and no firm footing, would take more out of us than four on a good road. Every nerve and muscle of our bodies was on the strain to keep our balance; and, added to this, the fear of falling is more exhausting than anything else. If the roads are very bad indeed, our shoes are roughed, but that makes us feel nervous at first.

When the weather was very bad, many of the men would go and sit in the tavern close by, and get someone to watch for them, but they often lost a fare in that way, and could not, as Jerry said, be there without spending money. He never went to the Rising Sun; there was a coffee shop near, where he now and then went, or he bought off an old man, who came to our rank with tins of hot coffee and pies. It was his opinion that spirits and beer made a man colder afterwards, and that dry clothes, good food, cheerfulness, and a comfortable wife at home were the best things to keep a cabman warm. Polly always supplied him with something to eat when he could not get home, and sometimes he would see little Dolly peeping from the corner of the street, to make sure if "father" was on the stand. If she saw him, she would run off at full speed and soon come back with something in a tin or basket, some hot soup or pudding that Polly had ready. It was wonderful how such a little thing could get safely across the street, often thronged with horses and carriages; but she was a brave little maid, and felt it quite an honor to bring "father's first course," as he used to call it. She was a general favorite on the stand, and there was not a man who would not have seen her safely across the street if Jerry had not been able to do it.

One cold, windy day, Dolly had brought Jerry a basin of something hot, and was standing by him whilst he ate it. He had scarcely begun when a gentleman, walking toward us very fast, held up his umbrella. Jerry touched his hat in return, gave the basin to Dolly, and was taking off my cloth, when the gentleman, hastening up, cried out, "*No, no, finish your soup, my friend;* I have not much time to spare, but I can wait till you have done, and set your little girl safe on the pavement." So saying, he seated himself in the cab. Jerry thanked him kindly, and came back to Dolly.

"*There, Dolly, that's a gentleman;* that's a real gentleman, Dolly. He has got time and thought for the comfort of a poor cabman and a little girl."

Jerry finished his soup, set the child across, and then took his orders to drive to Clapham Rise. Several times after that the same gentleman took our cab. I think he was very fond of dogs and horses, for whenever we took him to his own door, two or three dogs would come bounding out to meet him. Sometimes he came round and patted me, saying in his quiet, pleasant way, "This horse has got a good master, and he deserves it." It was a very rare thing for anyone to notice the horse that had been working for him. I have known ladies to do it now and then, and this gentleman and one or two others have given me a pat and a kind word; *but ninety-nine out of a hundred would as soon think of patting the steam engine that drew the train.*

This gentleman was not young, and there was a forward stoop in his shoulders as if he was always going at something. His lips were thin and close shut, though they had a very pleasant smile; his eye was keen, and there was something in his jaw and the motion of his head that made one think he was very determined in anything he set about. His voice was pleasant and kind; any horse would trust that voice, though it was just as decided as anything else about him.

One day he and another gentleman took our cab. They stopped at a shop in R—— Street, and while his friend went in, he stood at the door. A little ahead of us on the other side of the street, a cart with two very fine horses was standing before some wine vaults. The carter was not with them, and I cannot tell how long they had been standing, but they seemed to think they had waited long enough, and began to move off. Before they had gone many paces, the carter came running out and caught them. He seemed furious at their having moved, and with whip and rein punished them brutally, even beating them about the head. Our gentleman saw it all, and stepping quickly across the street, said in a decided voice:

"If you don't stop that directly, I'll have you summoned for leaving your horses, and for brutal conduct."

The man, who had clearly been drinking, poured forth some abusive language, but he left off knocking the horses about, and taking the reins, got into his cart. Meantime our friend had quietly taken out a notebook from his pocket, and looking at the name and address painted on the cart, he wrote something down.

"What do you want with that?" growled the carter, as he cracked his whip and was moving on. A nod and a grim smile was the only answer he got.

On returning to the cab, our friend was joined by his companion, who said laughingly, "I should have thought, Wright, you had enough business of your own to look after, without troubling yourself about other people's horses and servants."

Our friend stood still for a moment, and throwing his head a little back, said, "Do you know why this world is as bad as it is?"

"No," said the other.

"Then I'll tell you. *It is because people think only about their own business, and won't trouble themselves to stand up for the oppressed, nor bring the wrongdoer to light.* I never see a wicked thing like this without doing what I can, and many a master has thanked me for letting him know how his horses have been used."

"I wish there were more gentlemen like you, sir," said Jerry, "for they are wanted badly enough in this city."

After this we continued our journey, and as they got out of the cab, our friend was saying, "My doctrine is this, that *if we see cruelty or wrong that we have the power to stop, and do nothing, we make ourselves sharers in the guilt.*"

CHAPTER XXXIX

Seedy Sam

I SHOULD SAY THAT FOR A CAB HORSE I WAS VERY well off indeed; my driver was my owner, and it was in his interest to treat me well, and not overwork me, even had he not been so good a man as he was. But there were a great many horses which belonged to the large cab-owners, who let them out to their drivers for so much money a day. As the horses did not belong to these men, the only thing they thought of was how to get their money out of them—first, to pay the master, and then to provide for their own living, and a dreadful time some of these horses had of it. Of course I understood but little, but it was often talked over on the stand, and the Governor, who was a kind-hearted man, and fond of horses, would sometimes speak up if one came in very much jaded or ill-used.

One day, a shabby, miserable-looking driver, who went by the name of "Seedy Sam," brought in his horse looking dreadfully beat, and the Governor said:

"You and your horse look more fit for the police station than for this rank."

The man flung his tattered rug over the horse, turned full round upon the Governor, and said in a voice that sounded almost desperate:

"If the police have any business with the matter, it ought to be with the masters who charge us so much, or with the fares that are fixed so low. If a man has to pay eighteen shillings a day for the use of a cab and two horses, as many of us have to do in the season, and must make that up before we earn a penny for ourselves—I say, 'tis more than hard work: nine shillings a day to get out of each horse before you begin to get your own living. You know that's true, and if the horses don't work, we must starve, and I and my children have known what that is before now. I've six of 'em, and only one earns anything; I am on the stand fourteen or sixteen hours a day, and I haven't had a Sunday these ten or twelve weeks. You know, Skinner never gives a day if he can help it, and if I don't work hard, tell me who does? I want a warm coat and a mackintosh, but with so many to feed, how can a man get it? I had to pledge my clock a week ago to pay Skinner, and I shall never see it again."

Some of the other drivers stood round nodding their heads, and saying he was right. The man went on:

"You that have your own horses and cabs, or drive for good masters, have a chance of getting on and a chance of doing right; I haven't. We can't charge more than sixpence a mile after the first, within the four-mile radius. This very morning I had to go a clear six miles and only took three shillings. I could not get a return fare, and had to come all the way back; there's twelve miles for the horse and three shillings for me. After that I had a three-mile fare, and there were bags and boxes enough to have brought in a good many two-pences if they had been put outside, but you know how people do; all that could be piled up inside on the front seat were put in, and three heavy boxes went on the top. That was sixpence, and the fare one and sixpence; then I got a return for a shilling. Now, that makes eighteen miles for the horse and six shillings for me; there's three shillings still for that horse to earn, and nine shillings for the afternoon horse before I touch a penny.

"Of course it is not always as bad as that, but you know it often is, and I say 'tis a mockery to tell a man that he must not overwork his horse, for when a beast is downright tired there's nothing but the whip that will keep his legs a-going; you can't help yourself—you must put your wife and children before the horse. The master must look to that; we can't. I don't ill-use my horse for the sake of it; none of you can say I do. There's wrong lays somewhere—never a day's rest, never a quiet hour with the wife and children. I often feel like an old man, though I'm only forty-five. You know how quick some of the gentry are to suspect us of cheating and overcharging; why, they stand with their purses in their hands, counting it over to a penny, and looking at us as if we were pickpockets. I wish some of 'em had got to sit on my box sixteen hours a day, and get a living out of it and eighteen shillings beside, and that in all weathers; they would not be so uncommon particular never to give us a sixpence over, or to cram all the luggage inside. Of course, some of 'em tip us pretty handsome now and then, or else we could not live, but you can't *depend* upon that."

The men who stood round much approved this speech, and one of them said, "It is desperate hard, and if a man sometimes does what is wrong it is no wonder, and if he gets a dram too much, who's to blow him up?"

PLATE 9 *Jerry seemed quite as happy as I* (Page 172)

PLATE 10 *I'll drive you safe to the hospital* (Page 194)

PLATE 11 *New Year's Eve* (Page 203)

PLATE 12 *Down!* (Page 217)

Jerry had taken no part in this conversation, but I never saw his face look so sad before. The Governor had stood with both his hands in his pockets; now he took his handkerchief out of his hat, and wiped his forehead.

"You've beaten me, Sam," he said, "for it's all true, and I won't cast it up to you anymore about the police, it was the look in that horse's eye that came over me. *It is hard lines for man, and it is hard lines for beast,* and who's to mend it I don't know. But anyway you might tell the poor beast that you were sorry to take it out of him in that way. *Sometimes a kind word is all we can give 'em, poor brutes, and 'tis wonderful what they do understand.*"

A few mornings after this talk, a new man came on the stand with Sam's cab.

"Halloo!" said one. "What's up with Seedy Sam?"

"He's ill in bed," said the man. "He was taken last night in the yard, and could scarcely crawl home. His wife sent a boy this morning to say his father was in a high fever and could not get out; so I'm here instead."

The next morning the same man came again.

"How is Sam?" inquired the Governor.

"He's gone," said the man.

"What! Gone? You don't mean to say he's dead?"

"Just snuffed out," said the other. "He died at four o'clock this morning. All yesterday he was raving—raving about Skinner, and having no Sundays. 'I never had a Sunday's rest,' these were his last words."

No one spoke for a while, and then the Governor said, "I tell you what, mates, this is a warning for us."

CHAPTER XL

Poor Ginger

One day, whilst our cab and many others were waiting outside one of the parks where music was playing, a shabby old cab drove up beside ours. The horse was an old worn-out chestnut, with an ill-kept coat, and bones that showed plainly through it; the knees knuckled over, and the forelegs were very unsteady. I had been eating some hay, and the wind rolled a little of it that way, and the poor creature put out her long, thin neck and picked it up, and then turned around and looked about for more. There was a hopeless look in the dull eye that I could not help noticing, and then, as I was thinking where I had seen that horse before, she looked full at me and said, "Black Beauty, is that you?"

It was Ginger! But how changed! The beautifully arched and glossy neck was now straight and lank and fallen in; the clean, straight legs and delicate fetlocks were swelled; the joints were grown out of shape with hard work; the face, that was once so full of spirit and life was now full of suffering, and I could tell by the heaving of her sides, and her frequent cough, how bad her breath was.

Our drivers were standing together a little way off, so I sidled up to her a step or two that we might have a little quiet talk. It was a sad tale that she had to tell.

After a twelve-months' run-off at Earlshall, she was considered to be fit for work again, and was sold to a gentleman. For a little while she got on very well, but after a longer gallop than usual the old strain returned, and after being rested and doctored, she was again sold. In this way she changed hands several times, but always getting lower down.

"And so at last," said she, "I was bought by a man who keeps a number of cabs and horses, and lets them out. You look well off, and I am glad of it, but I could not tell you what my life has been. When they found out my weakness, they said I was not worth what they gave for me, *and that I must go into one of the low cabs, and just be used up.* That is what they are doing, whipping and working with never one thought of what I suffer—they paid for me, and must get it out of me, they say. The man who hires me now pays a deal of money to the owner every day, and so he has to get it out of me too; and so it's all the week round and round, with never a Sunday rest."

I said, "You used to stand up for yourself if you were ill-used."

"Ah!" she said. "I did once, but it's no use; men are strongest, and if they are cruel and have no feeling, there is nothing that we can do, but just bear it, bear it on and on to the end. I wish the end was come; I wish I was dead. I have seen dead horses, and I am sure they do not suffer pain. I wish I may drop down dead at my work, and not be sent off to the knacker's."

I was very much troubled, and I put my nose up to hers, but I could say nothing to comfort her. I think she was pleased to see me, for she said, "You are the only friend I ever had."

Just then her driver came up, and with a tug at her mouth, backed her out of the line and drove off, leaving me very sad indeed.

A short time after this, a cart with a dead horse in it passed our cab-stand. The head hung out of the cart-tail, the lifeless tongue was slowly dripping with blood, and the sunken eyes! But I can't speak of them; the sight was too dreadful. It was a chestnut horse with a long, thin neck. I saw a white streak down the forehead. I believe it was Ginger; I hoped it was, for then her troubles would be over. *Oh! if men were more merciful they would shoot us before we came to such misery.*

CHAPTER XLI

The Butcher

I SAW A GREAT DEAL OF TROUBLE AMONGST THE horses in London, and much of it that might have been prevented by a little common sense. We horses do not mind hard work if we are treated reasonably, and I am sure there are many driven by quite poor men who have a happier life than I had when I used to go in the Countess of W——'s carriage, with my silver-mounted harness and high feeding.

It often went to my heart to see how the little ponies were used, straining along with heavy loads, or staggering under heavy blows from some low, cruel boy. Once I saw a little gray pony with a thick mane and a pretty head, and so much like Merrylegs that if I had not been in harness I should have neighed to him. He was doing his best to pull a heavy cart while a strong, rough boy was cutting him under the belly with his whip, and chucking cruelly at his little mouth. Could it be Merrylegs? It was just like him; but then Mr.

Bloomfield was never to sell him, and I think he would not do it; but this might have been quite as good a little fellow and had as happy a place when he was young.

I often noticed the great speed at which butchers' horses were made to go, though I did not know why it was so, till one day when we had to wait some time in St. John's Wood. There was a butcher's shop next door, and as we were standing a butcher's cart came dashing up at a great pace. The horse was hot, and much exhausted; he hung his head down, while his heaving sides and trembling legs showed how hard he had been driven. The lad jumped out of the cart and was getting the basket, when the master came out of the shop much displeased. After looking at the horse, he turned angrily to the lad:

"How many times shall I tell you not to drive in this way? You ruined the last horse and broke his wind, and you are going to ruin this in the same way. If you were not my own son, I would dismiss you on the spot; it is a disgrace to have a horse brought to the shop in a condition like that. You are liable to be taken up by the police for such driving, and if you are, you need not look to me for bail, for I have spoken to you till I am tired; you must look out for yourself."

During this speech, the boy had stood by, sullen and dogged, but when his father ceased, he broke out angrily. It wasn't his fault, and he wouldn't take the blame; he was only going by orders all the time.

"You always say, 'Now be quick, now look sharp!' and when I go to the houses, one wants a leg of mutton for an early dinner, and I must be back with it in a quarter of an hour. Another cook had forgotten to order the beef; I must go and fetch it and be back in no time, or the mistress will scold; and the housekeeper says they have company coming unexpectedly, and must have some chops sent up directly; and the lady at No. 4, in the Crescent, *never* orders her dinner till the meat comes in for lunch; and it's nothing but hurry, hurry, all the time. *If the gentry would think of what they want, and order their meat the day before, there need not be this blow up!*"

"I wish to goodness they would," said the butcher. " 'Twould save me a wonderful deal of harass, and I could suit my customers much better if I knew beforehand—but there—what's the use of talking—who ever thinks of a butcher's convenience, or a butcher's horse? Now, then, take him in, and look to him well; mind he does not go out again today, and if anything else is wanted, you must carry it yourself in the basket." With that he went in, and the horse was led away.

But all boys are not cruel. I have seen some as fond of their pony or donkey as if it had been a favorite dog, and the little creatures have worked away as cheerfully and willingly for their young drivers as I work for Jerry. It may be hard work sometimes, but a friend's hand and voice make it easy.

There was a young coster-boy who came up our street with greens and potatoes; he had an old pony not very handsome, but the cheerfullest and pluckiest little thing I ever saw, and to see how fond those two were of each other was a treat. The pony followed his master like a dog, and when he got into his cart would trot off without a whip or a word, and rattle down the street as merrily as if he had come out of the Queen's stables. Jerry liked the boy, and called him "Prince Charlie," for he said he would make a king of drivers someday.

There was an old man, too, who used to come up our street with a little coal cart. He wore a coal-heaver's hat, and looked rough and black. He and his old horse used to plod together along the street, like two good partners who understood each other; the horse would stop of his own accord at the doors where they took coal of him; he used to keep one ear bent toward his master. The old man's cry could be heard up the street long before he came near. I never knew what he said, but the children called him "Old Ba-a-ar Hoo," for it sounded like that. Polly took her coal of him, and was very friendly, and Jerry said it was a comfort to think how happy an old horse *might* be in a poor place.

CHAPTER XLII

The Election

AS WE CAME INTO THE YARD ONE AFTERNOON, Polly came out.

"Jerry! I've had Mr. B—— here asking about your vote, and he wants to hire your cab for the election; he will call for an answer."

"Well, Polly, you may say that my cab will be otherwise engaged. I should not like to have it pasted over with their great bills, and as to making Jack and Captain race about to the public-houses to bring up half-drunken voters, why I think 'twould be an insult to the horses. No, I shan't do it."

"I suppose you'll vote for the gentleman? He said he was of your politics."

"So he is in some things, but I shall not vote for him, Polly; you know what his trade is?"

"Yes."

"Well, a man who gets rich by that trade may be all very well in some ways, but he is blind as to what working-men want. I could not in my conscience send him up to make the laws. I daresay they'll be angry, but every man must do what he thinks to be the best for his country."

On the morning before the election, Jerry was putting me into the shafts, when Dolly came into the yard sobbing and crying, with her little blue frock and white pinafore spattered all over with mud.

"Why, Dolly, what is the matter?"

"Those naughty boys," she sobbed, "have thrown the dirt all over me, and called me a little raga—raga—"

"They called her a little 'blue' ragamuffin, father," said Harry, who ran in looking very angry. "But I have given it to them. They won't insult my sister again. I have given them a thrashing they will remember; a set of cowardly, rascally 'orange' blackguards!"

Jerry kissed the child and said, "Run in to your mother, my pet, and tell her I think you had better stay at home today and help her."

Then turning gravely to Harry:

"My boy, I hope you will always defend your sister, and give anybody who insults her a good thrashing—that is as it should be; but mind, I won't have any election blackguarding on my premises. There are as many 'blue' blackguards as there are 'orange,' and as many white as there are purple, or any other color, and I won't have any of my family mixed up with it. Even women and children are ready to quarrel for the sake of a color, and not one in ten of them knows what it is about."

"Why, father, I thought blue was for Liberty."

"My boy, Liberty does not come from colors, they only show party; and all the liberty you can get out of them is liberty to get drunk at other people's expense, liberty to ride to the poll in a dirty old cab, liberty to abuse anyone that does not wear your color, and to shout yourself hoarse at what you only half understand—that's your liberty!"

"Oh, father, you are laughing."

"No, Harry, I am serious, and I am ashamed to see how men go on that ought to know better. An election is a very serious thing; at least it ought to be, and every man ought to vote according to his conscience, and let his neighbor do the same."

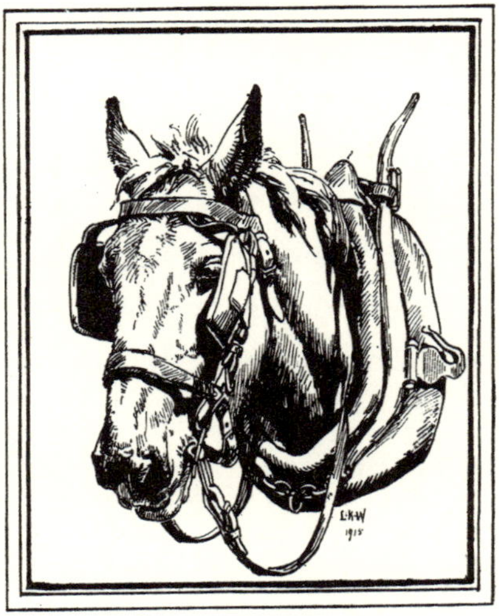

CHAPTER XLIII

A Friend in Need

AT LAST CAME THE ELECTION DAY; THERE WAS NO lack of work for Jerry and me. First came a stout, puffy gentleman with a carpet-bag; he wanted to go to Bishopsgate Station. Then we were called by a party who wished to be taken to the Regent's Park, and next we were wanted in a side street, where a timid, anxious old lady was waiting to be taken to the bank; there we had to stop to take her back again, and just as we had set her down a red-faced gentleman with a handful of papers came running up out of breath, and before Jerry could get down, he had opened the door, popped himself in, and called out, "Bow Street Police Station, quick!" So off we went with him, and when after another turn or two we came back, there was no other cab on the stand. Jerry put on my nose-bag, for as he said, "We must eat when we can on such days as these, so munch away, Jack, and make the best of your time, old boy."

I found I had a good feed of crushed oats wetted up with a little bran; this would be a treat any day, but was specially refreshing then. Jerry was so thoughtful and kind—what horse would not do his best for such a master? Then he took out one of Polly's meat pies, and standing near me, he began to eat it. The streets were very full, and the cabs, with the candidates' colors on them, were dashing about through the crowd as if life and limb were of no consequence. We saw two people knocked down that day, and one was a woman. The horses were having a bad time of it, poor things! But the voters inside thought nothing of that; many of them were half drunk, hurrahing out of the cab windows if their own party came by. It was the first election I had seen, and I don't want to be in another, though I have heard things are better now.

Jerry and I had not eaten many mouthfuls before a poor young woman carrying a heavy child came along the street. She was looking this way and that way, and seemed quite bewildered. Presently she made her way up to Jerry, and asked if he could tell her the way to St. Thomas's Hospital, and how far it was to get there. She had come from the country that morning, she said, in a market cart; she did not know about the election, and was quite a stranger in London. She had got an order for the hospital, for her little boy. The child was crying with a feeble, pining cry.

"Poor little fellow!" she said. "He suffers a deal of pain. He is four years old, and can't walk any more than a baby; but the doctor said if I could get him into the hospital, he might get well. Pray, sir, how far is it? And which way is it?"

"Why, missis," said Jerry, "you can't get there walking through crowds like this! Why, it is three miles away, and that child is heavy."

"Yes, bless him, he is; but I am strong, thank God, and if I knew the way, I think I should get on somehow. Please tell me the way."

"You can't do it," said Jerry, "you might be knocked down and the child be run over. Now, look here, just get into this cab, and I'll drive you safe to the hospital. Don't you see the rain is coming on?"

"No, sir, no; I can't do that, thank you; I have only just money enough to get back with. Please tell me the way."

"Look you here, missis," said Jerry, "I've got a wife and dear children at home, and I know a father's feelings. Now get you into that cab, and I'll take you there for nothing. I'd be ashamed of myself to let a woman and a sick child run a risk like that."

"Heaven bless you!" said the woman, and burst into tears.

"There, there, cheer up, my dear, I'll soon take you there; come, let me put you inside."

As Jerry went to open the door, two men, with colors in their hats and buttonholes, ran up, calling out, "Cab!"

"Engaged," cried Jerry, but one of the men, pushing past the woman, sprang into the cab, followed by the other. Jerry looked as stern as a policeman. "This cab is already engaged, gentlemen, by that lady."

"Lady!" said one of them. "Oh, she can wait! Our business is very important; besides we were in first, it is our right, and we shall stay in."

A droll smile came over Jerry's face as he shut the door upon them. "All right, gentlemen, pray stay in as long as it suits you. I can wait while you rest yourselves." And turning his back upon them, he walked up to the young woman, who was standing near me. "They'll soon be gone," he said, laughing. "Don't trouble yourself, my dear."

And they soon were gone, for when they understood Jerry's dodge they got out, calling him all sorts of bad names and blustering about his number and getting a summons. After this little stoppage we were soon on our way to the hospital, going as much as possible through by-streets. Jerry rang the great bell, and helped the young woman out.

"Thank you a thousand times," she said. "I could never have got there alone."

"You're kindly welcome, and I hope the dear child will soon be better."

He watched her go in at the door, and gently he said to himself, *"Inasmuch as ye have done it to one of the least of these."* Then he patted my neck, which was always his way when anything pleased him.

The rain was now coming down fast, and just as we were leaving the hospital the door opened again, and the porter called out, "Cab!" We stopped, and a lady came down the steps. Jerry seemed to know her at once; she put back her veil and said, "Barker! Jeremiah Barker! Is it you? I am very glad to find you here; you are just the friend I want, for it is very difficult to get a cab in this part of London today."

"I shall be proud to serve you, ma'am. I am right glad I happened to be here. Where may I take you to, ma'am?"

"To the Paddington Station, and then if we are in good time, as I think we shall be, you shall tell me all about Mary and the children."

We got to the station in good time, and being under shelter, the lady stood a good while talking to Jerry. I found she had been Polly's mistress, and after many inquiries about her, she said:

"How do you find the cab work suits you in winter? I know Mary was rather anxious about you last year."

"Yes, ma'am, she was. I had a bad cough that followed me up quite into the warm weather, and when I am kept out late, she does worry herself a good deal. You see, ma'am, it is all hours and all weathers, and that does try a man's constitution; but I am getting on pretty well, and I should feel quite lost if I had not horses to look after."

"Well, Barker," she said, "it would be a great pity that you should seriously risk your health in this work, not only for your own but for Mary's and the children's sake. There are many places where good drivers or good grooms are wanted, and if ever you think you ought to give up this cab work, let me know."

Then, sending some kind messages to Mary, she put something into his hand, saying, "There is five shillings each for the two children; Mary will know how to spend it."

Jerry thanked her and seemed much pleased, and turning out of the station, we at last reached home, and I, at least, was tired.

CHAPTER XLIV

Old Captain and His Successor

CAPTAIN AND I WERE GREAT FRIENDS. HE WAS A noble old fellow and was very good company. I never thought that he would have to leave his home and go down the hill, but his turn came, and this was how it happened. I was not there, but I heard all about it.

He and Jerry had taken a party to the great railway station over London Bridge, and were coming back, somewhere between the Bridge and the Monument, when Jerry saw a brewer's empty dray coming along, drawn by two powerful horses. The drayman was lashing his horses with his heavy whip; the dray was light, and they started off at a furious rate; the man had no control over them, and the street was full of traffic. One young girl was knocked down and run over, and the next moment they dashed up against our cab. Both the wheels were torn off and the cab was thrown over. Captain was dragged down, the shafts splintered, and one of them ran into his side. Jerry, too, was thrown, but was only bruised. Nobody could tell how he escaped; he always said it was a miracle. When poor Captain was got up, he was found to be very much cut and knocked about. Jerry led him home gently, and a sad sight it was to see the blood soaking into his white coat and dropping from his side and shoulder. *The drayman was proved to be very drunk,* and was fined, and the brewer had to pay damages to our master. But there was no one to pay damages to poor Captain.

The farrier and Jerry did the best they could to ease his pain and make him comfortable. The fly had to be mended, and for several days I did not go out, and Jerry earned nothing. The first time we went to the stand after the accident, the Governor came up to hear how Captain was.

"He'll never get over it," said Jerry, "at least not for my work, so the farrier said this morning. He says he may do for carting, and that sort of work. It has put me out very much. Carting, indeed! I've seen what horses come to at that work round London. I only wish all the drunkards could be put in a lunatic asylum, instead of being allowed to run foul of sober people. If they would break their *own* bones, and smash their *own* carts, and lame their *own* horses, that would be their own affair, and we might let them alone. But it seems to me that the innocent always suffer; and then they talk about compensation! You can't make compensation; there's all the trouble, and vexation, and loss of time, besides losing a good horse that's like an old friend—it's nonsense talking of compensation! *If there's one devil that I should like to see in the bottomless pit more than another, it's the drink devil.*"

"I say, Jerry," said the Governor, "you are treading pretty hard on my toes, you know; I'm not so good as you are, more shame for me; I wish I was."

"Well," said Jerry, "why don't you cut with it, Governor? You are too good a man to be the slave of such a thing."

"I'm a great fool, Jerry, but I tried once for two days, and I thought I should have died. How did you do it?"

"I had hard work at it for several weeks; you see I never did get drunk, but I found that I was not my own master, and that when the craving came on, it was hard work to say 'no.' I saw that one of us must knock under, the drink devil or Jerry Barker, and I said that it should not be Jerry Barker, God helping me. But it was a struggle, and I wanted all the help I could get, for till I tried to break the habit, I did not know how strong it was. But then Polly took such pains that I should have good food, and when the craving came on, I used to get a cup of coffee, or some peppermint, or read a bit in my book, and that was a help to me. Sometimes I had to say over and over to myself, 'Give up the drink or lose your soul! Give up the drink or break Polly's heart!' But thanks be to God and my dear wife, my chains were broken, and now for ten years I have not tasted a drop, and never wish for it."

"I've a great mind to try at it," said Grant, "for 'tis a poor thing not to be one's own master."

"Do, Governor, do, you'll never repent it; and what a help it would be to some of the poor fellows in our rank if they saw you do without it. I know there's two or three would like to keep out of that tavern if they could."

At first Captain seemed to do well, but he was a very old horse, and it was only his wonderful constitution and Jerry's care that had kept him up at the cab work so long; now he broke down very much. The farrier said he might mend up enough to sell for a few pounds, but Jerry said no! A few pounds got by selling a good old servant into hard work and misery would canker all the rest of his money, and he thought the kindest thing he could do for the fine old fellow would be to put a sure bullet through his head, and then he would never suffer more, for he did not know where to find a kind master for the rest of his days.

The day after this was decided, Harry took me to the forge for some shoes. When I returned, Captain was gone. I and the family all felt it very much.

Jerry had now to look out for another horse, and he soon heard of one through an acquaintance who was under-groom in a nobleman's stables. He was a valuable young horse, but he had run away, smashed into another carriage, flung his lordship out, and so cut and blemished himself that he was no longer fit for a gentleman's stables, and the coachman had orders to look round and sell him as well as he could.

"I can do with high spirits," said Jerry, "if a horse is not vicious or hard-mouthed."

"There is not a bit of vice in him," said the man. "His mouth is very tender, and I think myself that was the cause of the accident. You see he had just been clipped, and the weather was bad, and he had not had exercise enough, and when he did go out, he was as full of spring as a balloon. Our governor (the coachman, I mean) had him harnessed in as tight and strong as he could, with the martingale and the check-rein, a very sharp curb, and the reins put in at the bottom bar. It is my belief that it made the horse mad, being tender in the mouth and so full of spirit."

"Likely enough; I'll come see him," said Jerry.

The next day Hotspur—that was his name—came home. He was a fine brown horse, without a white hair in him, as tall as Captain, with a very handsome head, and only five years old. I gave him a friendly greeting by way of good fellowship, but did not ask him any questions. The first night he was very restless. Instead of lying down, he kept jerking his halter rope up and down through the ring, and knocking the block about against the manger, so that I could not sleep. However, the next day, after five or six hours in the cab, he came in quiet and sensible. Jerry patted and talked to him a good deal, and very soon they understood each other, and Jerry said that with an easy bit and plenty of work he would be as gentle as a lamb; and that it was an ill wind that blew nobody good, for if his lordship had lost a hundred-guinea favorite, the cabman had gained a good horse with all his strength in him.

Hotspur thought it a great come-down to be a cab horse, and was disgusted at standing in the rank, but he confessed to me at the end of the week that an easy mouth and a free head made up for a great deal, and, after all, the work was not so degrading as having one's head and tail fastened to each other at the saddle. In fact, he settled in well, and Jerry liked him very much.

CHAPTER XLV

Jerry's New Year

CHRISTMAS AND THE NEW YEAR ARE VERY MERRY times for some people, but for cabmen and cabmen's horses it is no holiday, though it may be a harvest. There are so many parties, balls, and places of amusement open that the work is hard and often late. Sometimes driver and horse have to wait for hours in the rain or frost, shivering with cold, while the merry people within are dancing away to the music. *I wonder if the beautiful ladies ever think of the weary cabman waiting on his box, and his patient beast standing till his legs get stiff with cold.*

I had now most of the evening work, as I was well accustomed to standing, and Jerry was also more afraid of Hotspur taking cold. We had a great deal of late work in the Christmas week, and Jerry's cough was bad; but, however late we were, Polly sat up for him, and came out with the lantern to meet him, looking anxious and troubled.

On the evening of the New Year we had to take two gentlemen to a house in one of the West End squares. We set them down at nine o'clock, and were told to come again at eleven. "But," said one of them, "as it is a card party, you may have to wait a few minutes, but don't be late." As the clock struck eleven we were at the door, for Jerry was always punctual. The clock chimed the quarters—one, two, three, and then struck twelve, but the door did not open.

The wind had been very changeable, with squalls of rain during the day, but now it came on sharp, driving sleet, which seemed to come all the way round. It was very cold, and there was no shelter. Jerry got off his box and came and pulled one of my cloths a little more over my neck; then he took a turn or two up and down, stamping his feet; then he began to beat his arms, but that set him off coughing, so he opened the cab door and sat at the bottom with his feet on the pavement, and was a little sheltered. Still the clock chimed the quarters, and no one came. At half-past twelve he rang the bell and asked the servant if he would be wanted that night.

"Oh, yes, you'll be wanted safe enough," said the man; "you must not go; it will soon be over." And again Jerry sat down, but his voice was so hoarse I could hardly hear him.

At a quarter-past one the door opened, and the two gentlemen came out. They got into the cab without a word, and told Jerry where to drive; that was nearly two miles. My legs were numb with cold, and I thought I should have stumbled. When the men got out they never said they were sorry to have kept us waiting so long, but were angry at the charge. However, as Jerry never charged more than was his due, so he never took less; and they had to pay for the two hours and a quarter waiting; but it was hard-earned money to Jerry.

At last we got home. He could hardly speak, and his cough was dreadful. Polly asked no questions, but opened the door and held the lantern for him.

"Can't I do something?" she said.

"Yes, get Jack something warm, and then boil me some gruel."

This was said in a hoarse whisper; he could hardly get his breath, but he gave me a rub down, as usual, and even went up into the hayloft for an extra bundle of straw for my bed. Polly brought me a warm mash that made me comfortable, and then they locked the door.

It was late the next morning before anyone came, and then it was only Harry. He cleaned us and fed us, and swept out the stalls, then he put the straw back again as if it was Sunday. He was very still, and neither whistled nor sang. At noon he came again and gave us our food and water. This time Dolly came with him; she was crying, and I could gather from what they said that Jerry was dangerously ill, and the doctor said it was a bad case. So two days passed, and there was great trouble indoors. We only saw Harry, and sometimes Dolly. I think she came for company, for Polly was always with Jerry, and he had to be kept very quiet.

On the third day, while Harry was in the stable, a tap came at the door, and Governor Grant came in.

"I wouldn't go to the house, my boy," he said, "but I want to know how your father is."

"He is very bad," said Harry. "He can't be much worse; they call it 'bronchitis.' The doctor thinks it will turn one way or another tonight."

"That's bad, very bad," said Grant, shaking his head. "I know two men who died of that last week; it takes 'em off in no time. But while there's life there's hope, so you must keep up your spirits."

"Yes," said Harry, quickly, "and the doctor said that father had a better chance than most men, because he didn't drink. He said yesterday the fever was so high that if father had been a drinking man it would have burnt him up like a piece of paper; but I believe he thinks he will get over it. Don't you think he will, Mr. Grant?"

The Governor looked puzzled.

"If there's any rule that good men should get over these things, I am sure he will, my boy; he's the best man I know. I'll look in early tomorrow."

Early next morning he was there.

"Well?" said he.

"Father is better," said Harry. "Mother hopes he will get over it."

"Thank God!" said the Governor. "And now you must keep him warm, and keep his mind easy, and that brings me to the horses. You see, Jack will be all the better for the rest of the week or two in a warm stable, and you can easily take him a turn up and down the street to stretch his legs. But his young one, if he does not get to work, he will soon be all up on end, as you may say, and will be rather too much for you; and when he does go out, there'll be an accident."

"It is like that now," said Harry. "I have kept him short of corn, but he's so full of spirit I don't know what to do with him."

"Just so," said Grant. "Now, look here. Will you tell your mother that, if she is agreeable, I will come for him every day till something is arranged, and take him for a good spell of work, and whatever he earns, I'll bring your mother half of it, and that will help with the horses' feed. Your father is in a good club, I know, but that won't keep the horses, and they'll be eating their heads off all this time.

I'll come at noon and hear what she says." And without waiting for Harry's thanks, he was gone.

At noon I think he went and saw Polly, for he and Harry came to the stable together, harnessed Hotspur, and took him out.

For a week or more he came for Hotspur, and when Harry thanked him or said anything about his kindness, he laughed it off, saying it was all good luck for him, for his horses were wanting a little rest, which they would not otherwise have had.

Jerry grew better steadily, but the doctor said that he must never go back to the cab work again if he wished to be an old man. The children had many consultations together about what father and mother would do, and how they could help to earn money.

One afternoon Hotspur was brought in very wet and dirty. "The streets are nothing but slush," said the Governor. "It will give you a good warming, my boy, to get him clean and dry."

"All right, Governor," said Harry, "I shall not leave him till he is; you know I have been trained by my father."

"I wish all the boys had been trained like you," said the Governor.

While Harry was sponging off the mud from Hotspur's body and legs, Dolly came in, looking very full of something.

"Who lives at Fairstowe, Harry? Mother has got a letter from Fairstowe. She seemed so glad, and ran upstairs to father with it."

"Don't you know? Why, it is the name of Mrs. Fowler's place—mother's old mistress, you know—the lady that father met last summer, who sent you and me five shillings each."

"Oh! Mrs. Fowler. Of course I know all about her. I wonder what she is writing to mother about."

"Mother wrote to her last week," said Harry. "You know she

told father if ever he gave up the cab work she would like to know. I wonder what she says. Run in and see, Dolly."

Harry scrubbed away at Hotspur with a huish! huish! like any old ostler. In a few minutes Dolly came dancing into the stable.

"Oh, Harry, there never was anything so beautiful; Mrs. Fowler says we are all to go and live near her. There is a cottage now empty that will just suit us, with a garden, and a hen-house and apple-trees and everything! And her coachman is going away in the spring, and then she will want father in his place. And there are good families round, where you can get a place in the garden, or the stable, or as a page boy; and there's a good school for me; and mother is laughing and crying by turns, and father does look *so* happy!"

"That's uncommon jolly," said Harry, "and just the right thing, I should say. It will suit father and mother both; but I don't intend to be a page boy with tight clothes and rows of buttons. I'll be a groom or a gardener."

It was quickly settled that as soon as Jerry was well enough, they should remove to the country, and that the cab and horses should be sold as soon as possible.

This was heavy news for me, for I was not young now, and could not look for any improvement in my condition. Since I left Birtwick I had never been so happy as with my dear master Jerry; but three years of cab work, even under the best conditions, will tell on one's strength, and I felt I was not the horse that I had been.

Grant said at once that he would take Hotspur, and there were men on the stand who would have bought me, but Jerry said I should not go to cab work again with just anybody, and the Governor promised to find a place for me where I should be comfortable.

The day came for going away. Jerry had not been allowed to go out yet, and I never saw him after that New Year's eve. Polly and the children came to bid me goodbye. "Poor old Jack! Dear old Jack! I wish we could take you with us," she said, and then laying her hand on my mane, she put her face close to my neck and kissed me. Dolly was crying and kissed me too. Harry stroked me a great deal, but said nothing, only he seemed very sad, and so I was led away to my new place.

Part Four

CHAPTER XLVI

Jakes and the Lady

I WAS SOLD TO A CORN DEALER AND BAKER, WHOM Jerry knew, and with him he thought I should have good food and fair work. In the first he was quite right, and if my master had always been on the premises I do not think I should have been overloaded; but there was a foreman who was always hurrying and driving everyone, and frequently when I had quite a full load he would order something else to be taken on. My carter, whose name was Jakes, often said it was more than I ought to take, but the other always overruled him. " 'Twas no use going twice when once would do, and he chose to get business forward."

Jakes, like the other carters, always *had the check-rein up,* which prevented me from drawing easily, and by the time I had been there three or four months I found the work telling very much on my strength.

One day I was loaded more than usual, and part of the road was a steep uphill. I used all my strength, but I could not get on, and was obliged continually to stop. This vexed my driver, and he laid his whip on badly. "Get on, you lazy fellow," he said, "or I'll make you."

Again I started the heavy load and struggled on a few yards; again the whip came down, and again I struggled forward. The pain of that great cart whip was sharp, but my mind was hurt quite as much as my poor sides. To be punished and abused when I was doing my very best was so hard it took the heart out of me. A third time he was flogging me cruelly when a lady stepped quickly up to him and said in a sweet, earnest voice:

"Oh, pray do not whip your good horse any more; I am sure he is doing all he can, and the road is very steep; I am sure he is doing his best."

"If doing his best won't get this load up, he must do something more than his best; that's all I know, ma'am," said Jakes.

"But is it not a very heavy load?" she said.

"Yes, yes, too heavy," he said, "but that's not my fault. The foreman came just as we were starting, and would have three hundredweight more put on to save him trouble, and I must get on with it as well as I can."

He was raising the whip again, when the lady said:

"Pray, stop; I think I can help you if you will let me."

The man laughed.

"You see," she said, "you do not give him a fair chance; he cannot use all his power with his head held back as it is with that check-rein. If you would take it off, I am sure he would do better—*do* try it," she said persuasively. "I should be very glad if you would."

"Well, well," said Jakes, with a short laugh, "anything to please a lady, of course. How far would you wish it down, ma'am?"

"Quite down, give him his head altogether."

The rein was taken *off,* and in a moment I put my head down to my very knees. What a comfort it was! Then I tossed it up and down several times to get the aching stiffness out of my neck.

"Poor fellow, that is what you wanted!" said she, patting and stroking me with her gentle hand. "And now if you will speak kindly to him and lead him on, I believe he will be able to do better."

Jakes took the rein. "Come on, Blackie." I put down my head and threw my whole weight against the collar; I spared no strength; the load moved on, and I pulled it steadily up the hill, and then stopped to take breath.

The lady had walked along the footpath, and now came across into the road. She stroked and patted my neck, as I had not been patted for many a long day.

"You see he was quite willing when you gave him the chance. I am sure he is a fine-tempered creature, and I dare say he has known better days. You won't put that rein on again, will you?" For he was just going to hitch it up on the old plan.

"Well, ma'am, I can't deny that having his head has helped him up the hill, and I'll remember it another time, and thank you, ma'am; but if he went without a check-rein I should be the laughing-stock of all the carters; it is the fashion, you see."

"Is it not better," she said, "to lead a good fashion than to follow a bad one? A great many gentlemen do not use check-reins now; our carriage horses have not worn them for fifteen years, and work with much less fatigue than those who have them. Besides," she added in a very serious voice, "we have no right to distress any of God's creatures without a very good reason. We call them dumb animals, and so they are, for they cannot tell us how they feel, but they do not suffer less because they have no words. But I must not detain you now; I thank you for trying my plan with your good horse, and I am sure you will find it far better than the whip. Good-day." And with another soft pat on my neck, she stepped lightly across the path, and I saw her no more.

"That was a real lady, I'll be bound for it," said Jakes to himself. "She spoke just as polite as if I was a gentleman, and I'll try her plan, uphill, at any rate." And I must do him the justice to say that he let my rein out several holes, and going uphill after that he always gave me my head; but the heavy loads went on. Good feed and fair rest will keep one's strength under full work; *but no horse can stand against overloading,* and I was getting so thoroughly pulled down from this cause that a younger horse was bought in my place. I may as well mention here what I suffered at this time from another cause. I had heard horses speak of it, but had never myself had experience of the evil; *this was a badly lighted stable.* There was only one very small window at the end, and the consequence was that the stalls were almost dark.

Besides the depressing effect this had on my spirits, it very much weakened my sight, and when I was suddenly brought out of the darkness into the glare of daylight, it was very painful to my eyes. Several times I stumbled over the threshold, and could scarcely see where I was going.

I believe, had I stayed there very long, I should have become purblind, and that would have been a great misfortune, for I have heard men say that a stone-blind horse was safer to drive than one which had imperfect sight, as it generally makes them very timid. However, I escaped without any permanent injury to my sight, and was sold to a large cab owner.

CHAPTER XLVII

Hard Times

I SHALL NEVER FORGET MY NEW MASTER. HE HAD black eyes and a hooked nose, his mouth was as full of teeth as a bulldog's and his voice was as harsh as the grinding of cart wheels over gravel stones. His name was Nicholas Skinner, and I believe he was the same man that poor Seedy Sam drove for.

I have heard men say that seeing is believing, but I should say that *feeling* is believing; for much as I had seen before, I never knew till now the utter misery of a cab horse's life.

Skinner had a low set of cabs and a low set of drivers; he was hard on the men, and the men were hard on the horses. In this place we had no Sunday rest, and it was in the heat of summer.

Sometimes on a Sunday morning, a party of fast men would hire the cab for the day, four of them inside and another with the driver, and I had to take them ten or fifteen miles out into the country, and back again. *Never would any of them get down to walk up a hill,* let it be ever so steep, or the day ever so hot—unless, indeed, the driver was afraid I should not manage it, and sometimes I was so fevered and worn that I could hardly touch my food. How I used to long for the nice bran mash with niter in it that Jerry used to give us on Saturday nights in hot weather that used to cool us down and make us so comfortable. Then we had two nights and a whole day for unbroken rest, and on Monday morning we were as fresh as young horses again; but here there was no rest, and my driver was just as hard as his master. He had a cruel whip with something so sharp at the end that it sometimes drew blood, and he would even whip me under the belly, and flip the lash out at my head. Indignities like these took the heart out of me terribly, but still I did my best and never hung back, for, as poor Ginger said, it was no use; men are the strongest.

My life was now so utterly wretched that I wished I might, like Ginger, drop down dead at my work, and be out of my misery, and one day my wish very nearly came to pass.

I went on the stand at eight in the morning, and had done a good share of work, when we had to take a fare to the railway. A long train was just expected in, so my driver pulled up at the back of some of the outside cabs, to take the chance of a return fare. It was a very heavy train, and as all the cabs were soon engaged, ours was called for. There was a party of four; a noisy, blustering man with a lady, a little boy, and a young girl, and a great deal of luggage. The lady and the boy got into the cab, and while the man ordered about the luggage, the young girl came and looked at me.

"Papa," she said, "I am sure this poor horse cannot take us and all our luggage so far, he is so very weak and worn out. Do look at him."

"Oh, he's all right, miss," said my driver, "he's strong enough."

The porter, who was pulling about some heavy boxes, suggested to the gentleman, as there was so much luggage, whether he would not take a second cab.

"Can your horse do it, or can't he?" said the blustering man.

"Oh! He can do it all right, sir; Send up the boxes, porter; he could take more than that." And he helped to haul up a box so heavy that I could feel the springs go down.

"Papa, papa, do take a second cab," said the young girl in a beseeching tone. "I am sure we are wrong, I am sure it is very cruel."

"Nonsense, Grace, get in at once, and don't make all this fuss. A pretty thing it would be if a man of business had to examine every cab-horse before he hired it—the man knows his own business of course. There, get in and hold your tongue!"

My gentle friend had to obey; and box after box was dragged up and lodged on the top of the cab, or settled by the side of the driver. At last all was ready, and with his usual jerk at the rein, and slash of the whip, he drove out of the station.

The load was very heavy, and I had had neither food nor rest since the morning; but I did my best, as I always had done, in spite of cruelty and injustice.

I got along fairly till we came to Ludgate Hill, but there the heavy load and my own exhaustion were too much. I was struggling to keep on, goaded by constant chucks of the rein and use of the whip, when, in a single moment—I cannot tell how—my feet slipped from under me, and I fell heavily to the ground on my side. The suddenness and the force with which I fell seemed to beat all the breath out of my body. I lay perfectly still; indeed, I had no power to move, and I thought now I was going to die. I heard a sort of confusion round me, loud, angry voices, and the getting down of the luggage, but it was all like a dream. I thought I heard that sweet, pitiful voice saying, "Oh, that poor horse! It is all our fault." Someone came and loosened the throat strap of my bridle, and undid the traces which kept the collar so tight upon me. Someone said, "He's dead, he'll never get up again." Then I could hear the policeman giving orders, but I did not even open my eyes; I could only draw a gasping breath now and then. Some cold water was thrown over my head, and some cordial was poured into my mouth, and something was covered over me. I cannot tell how long I lay there, but I found my life coming back, and a kind-voiced man was patting me and encouraging me to rise. After some more cordial had been given me, and after one or two attempts, I staggered to my feet, and was gently led to some stables which were close by. Here I was put into a well-littered stall, and some warm gruel was brought to me, which I drank thankfully.

In the evening I was sufficiently recovered to be led back to Skinner's stables, where I think they did the best for me they could. In the morning Skinner came with a farrier to look at me. He examined me very closely and said:

"This is a case of overwork more than disease, and if you could give him a run off for six months he would be able to work again; but now there is not an ounce of strength in him."

"Then he must just go to the dogs," said Skinner. "I have no meadows to nurse sick horses in—he might get well or he might not; that sort of thing don't suit my business. *My plan is to work 'em as long as they'll go, and then sell 'em for what they'll fetch at the knacker's or elsewhere.*"

"If he was broken-winded," said the farrier, "you had better have him killed out of hand, but he is not. There is a sale of horses coming off in about ten days; if you rest him and feed him up, he may pick up, and you may get more than his skin is worth, at any rate."

Upon this advice, Skinner, rather unwillingly, I think, gave orders that I should be well fed and cared for, and the stableman, happily for me, carried out the orders with a much better will than his master had in giving them. Ten days of perfect rest, plenty of good oats, hay, bran mashes, with boiled linseed mixed in them, did more to get up my condition than anything else could have done. Those linseed mashes were delicious, and I began to think, after all, it might be better to live than go to the dogs. When the twelfth day after the accident came, I was taken to the sale, a few miles out of London. I felt that any change from my present place must be an improvement.

CHAPTER XLVIII

Farmer Thoroughgood and His Grandson Willie

AT THIS SALE, OF COURSE, I FOUND MYSELF IN company with the old broken-down horses—some lame, some broken-winded, some old, and some that I am sure it would have been merciful to shoot.

The buyers and sellers, too, many of them, looked not much better off than the poor beasts they were bargaining about. There were poor old men, trying to get a horse or a pony for a few pounds that might drag about some little wood or coal cart. There were poor men trying to sell a worn-out beast for two or three pounds, rather than have the greater loss of killing him. Some of them looked as if poverty and hard times had hardened them all over; but there were others that I would have willingly used the last of my strength in serving; poor and shabby, but kind and humane, with voices that I could trust. There was one tottering old man that took a great fancy to me, and I to him, but I was not strong enough—it was an anxious time! Coming from the better part of the fair, I noticed a man who looked like a gentleman farmer, with a young boy by his side; he had a broad back and round shoulders, a kind, ruddy face, and he wore a broad-brimmed hat. When he came up to me and my companions, he gave a pitiful look round upon us. I saw his eye rest on me; I had still a good mane and tail, which did something for my appearance. I pricked my ears and looked at him.

"There's a horse, Willie," he said, "that has known better days."

"Poor old fellow!" said the boy. "Do you think, grandpapa, he was ever a carriage horse?"

"Oh, yes! my boy," said the farmer, coming closer. "He might have been anything when he was young; look at his nostrils and his ears, the shape of his neck and shoulders; there's a deal of breeding about that horse." He put out his hand and gave me a kind pat on the neck. I put out my nose in answer to his kindness; the boy stroked my face.

"Poor old fellow! See, grandpapa, how well he understands kindness. Could not you buy him and make him young again, as you did with Ladybird?"

"My dear boy, I can't make all old horses young; besides, Ladybird was not so very old, as she was run down and badly used."

"Well, grandpapa, I don't believe that this one is old, look at his mane and tail. I wish you would look into his mouth, and then you could tell; though he is so very thin, his eyes are not sunk like some old horses'."

The old gentleman laughed. "Bless the boy! He is as horsey as his old grandfather."

"But do look at his mouth and ask the price; I am sure he would grow young in our meadows."

The man who had brought me for sale now put in his word.

"The young gentleman's a real knowing one, sir. Now the fact is, this 'ere hoss is just pulled down with overwork in the cabs; he's not an old one, and I heerd as how the vetenary should say that a six months' run off would set him right up, being as how his wind was not broken. I've had the tending of him these ten days past, and a gratefuller, pleasanter animal I never met with, and 'twould be worth a gentleman's while to give a five-pound note for him and let him have a chance. I'll be bound he'd be worth twenty pounds next spring."

The old gentleman laughed and the little boy looked up eagerly.

"Oh, grandpapa, did you not say the colt sold for five pounds more than you expected? You would not be poorer if you did buy this one."

The farmer slowly felt my legs, which were much swelled and strained; then he looked at my mouth. "Thirteen or fourteen, I should say. Just trot him out, will you?"

I arched my poor thin neck, raised my tail a little, and threw out my legs as well as I could, for they were very stiff.

"What is the lowest you will take for him?" said the farmer as I came back.

"Five pounds, sir; that was the lowest price my master set."

" 'Tis a speculation," said the old gentleman, shaking his head, but at the same time slowly drawing out his purse, "quite a speculation! Have you any more business here?" he said, counting the sovereigns into his hand.

"No, sir; I can take him to the inn, if you please."

"Do so; I am now going there."

They walked forward, and I was led behind. The boy could hardly control his delight, and the old gentleman seemed to enjoy his pleasure. I had a good feed at the inn, and was then gently ridden home by a servant of my new master's, and turned into a large meadow with a shed in one corner of it.

Mr. Thoroughgood, for that was the name of my benefactor, gave orders that I should have hay and oats every night and morning, and the run of the meadow during the day; and, "You, Willie," said he, "must take the oversight of him; I give him in charge to you."

The boy was proud of his charge, and undertook it in all seriousness. There was not a day when he did not pay me a visit; sometimes picking me out among the other horses and giving me a bit of carrot, or something good, or sometimes standing by me while I ate my oats. He always came with kind words and caresses, and of course I grew very fond of him. He called me Old Crony, as I used to come to him in the field and follow him about. Sometimes he brought his grandfather, who always looked closely at my legs.

"This is our point, Willie," he would say. "But he is improving so steadily that I think we shall see a change for the better in the spring."

The perfect rest, the good food, the soft turf and exercise soon began to tell on my condition and my spirits. I had a good constitution from my mother and I was never strained when I was young, so that I had a better chance than many horses who have been worked before they came to their full strength. During the winter my legs improved so much that I began to feel quite young again. The spring came around, and one day in March Mr. Thoroughgood determined that he would try me in the phaeton. I was well pleased, and he and Willie drove me a few miles. My legs were not stiff now, and I did the work with perfect ease.

"He's growing young, Willie. We must give him a little gentle work now, and by midsummer he will be as good as Ladybird. He has a beautiful mouth, and good paces; they can't be better."

"Oh, grandpapa, how glad I am you bought him!"

"So am I, my boy, but he has to thank you more than me; we must now be looking out for a quiet, genteel place for him, where he will be valued."

CHAPTER XLIX

My Last Home

ONE DAY DURING THIS SUMMER THE GROOM cleaned and dressed me with such extraordinary care that I thought some new change must be at hand. He trimmed my fetlocks and legs, passed the tarbush over my hoofs, and even parted my forelock. I think the harness had an extra polish. Willie seemed half anxious, half merry, as he got into the chaise with his grandfather.

"If the ladies take to him," said the old gentleman, "they'll be suited, and he'll be suited; we can but try."

At the distance of a mile or two from the village we came to a pretty, low house, with a lawn and shrubbery at the front and a drive up to the door. Willie rang the bell and asked if Miss Bloomfield or Miss Ellen was at home. Yes, they were. So, while Willie stayed with me, Mr. Thoroughgood went into the house. In about ten minutes he returned, followed by three ladies; one tall, pale lady, wrapped in a white shawl, leaned on a younger lady, with dark eyes and a merry face; the other, a very stately looking person, was Miss Bloomfield. They all came and looked at me and asked questions. The young lady—that was Miss Ellen—took to me very much; she said she was sure she should like me, I had such a good face. The tall, pale lady said she should always be nervous in riding behind a horse that had once been down, as I might come down again, and if I did she should never get over the fright.

"You see, ladies," said Mr. Thoroughgood, "many first-rate horses have had their knees broken through the carelessness of their drivers, without any fault of their own, and from what I see of this horse I should say that is his case; but, of course, I do not wish to influence you. If you incline, you can have him on trial, and then your coachman will see what he thinks of him."

"You have always been such a good adviser to us about our horses," said the stately lady, "that your recommendation would go a long way with me, and if my sister Lavinia sees no objection, we will accept your offer of a trial, with thanks."

It was then arranged that I should be sent for the next day.

In the morning a smart-looking young man came for me. At first he looked pleased, but when he saw my knees he said in a disappointed voice:

"I didn't think, sir, you would have recommended my ladies a blemished horse like that."

"Handsome is that handsome does," said my master. "You are only taking him on trial, and I am sure you will do fairly by him, young man, and if he is not as safe as any horse you ever drove, send him back."

I was led home, placed in a comfortable stable, fed, and left to myself. The next day, when my groom was cleaning my face, he said:

"That is just like the star that Black Beauty had; he is much the same height, too; I wonder where he is now."

A little further on he came to the place in my neck where I was bled, and where a little knot was left in the skin. He almost started, and began to look me over carefully, talking to himself.

"White star in the forehead, one white foot on the off side, this little knot just in that place"—then looking at the middle of my back—"and as I am alive, there is that little patch of white hair that John used to call 'Beauty's three-penny bit.' It *must* be Black Beauty! Why, Beauty! Beauty! Do you know me? Little Joe Green that almost killed you?" And he began patting and patting me as if he was quite overjoyed.

I could not say that I remembered him, for now he was a fine grown young fellow, with black whiskers and a man's voice, but I was sure he knew me, and that he was Joe Green, and I was very glad. I put my nose up to him, and tried to say that we were friends. I never saw a man so pleased.

"Give you a fair trial! I should think so indeed! I wonder who the rascal was that broke your knees, my old Beauty! You must have been badly served out somewhere. Well, well, it won't be my fault if you haven't good times of it now. I wish John Manly was here to see you."

In the afternoon I was put into a low park chair and brought to the door. Miss Ellen was going to try me, and Green went with her. I soon found that she was a good driver, and she seemed pleased with my paces. I heard Joe telling her about me, and that he was sure I was Squire Gordon's old "Black Beauty."

When we returned, the other sisters came out to hear how I had behaved myself. She told them what she had just heard, and said:

"I shall certainly write to Mrs. Gordon and tell her that her favorite horse has come to us. How pleased she will be!"

After this I was driven every day for a week or so, and as I appeared to be quite safe, Miss Lavinia at last ventured out in the small close carriage. After this it was quite decided to keep me and call me by my old name of "Black Beauty."

I have now lived in this happy place a whole year. Joe is the best and kindest of grooms. My work is easy and pleasant, and I feel my strength and spirits all coming back again. Mr. Thoroughgood said to Joe the other day:

"In your place he will last till he is twenty years old—perhaps more."

Willie always speaks to me when he can, and treats me as his special friend. *My ladies have promised that I shall never be sold,* and so I have nothing to fear; and here my story ends. My troubles are all over, and I am at home. And often before I am quite awake, I fancy I am still in the orchard at Birtwick, standing with my old friends under the apple trees.